This is war!

What was getting into everybody in River Heights? Was it just the reenactment turning them against one another? If things went on like this, pretty soon we'd have another war on our hands!

"You've gotten used to running everything in this town, lady," Jeffries told Mrs. Mahoney, getting more belligerent by the second. "Well, here's one thing you can't run. Me and my guys have put a lot of effort into this battle already, and we aren't taking orders from the likes of you."

"But . . . the whole idea of the reenactment was mine in the first place!" Mrs. Mahoney spluttered.

"Tough luck," Jeffries shot back. "You can mess around with your little picnic all you want, but leave the battle plans to us menfolk." He leaned over, breathing hotly in her face. *"Or else."*

NANCY DREW
girl detective™

#1 Without a Trace

#2 A Race Against Time

#3 False Notes

#4 High Risk

#5 Lights, Camera . . .

#6 Action!

#7 The Stolen Relic

#8 The Scarlet Macaw Scandal

#9 Secret of the Spa

#10 Uncivil Acts

Available from Aladdin Paperbacks

NANCY DREW

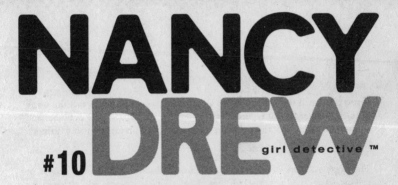

DREW
girl detective ™

#10

Uncivil Acts

CAROLYN KEENE

Aladdin Paperbacks
New York   London   Toronto   Sydney

❧ ALADDIN PAPERBACKS
An imprint of Simon & Schuster Children's Publishing Division
1230 Avenue of the Americas, New York, NY 10020
Copyright © 2005 by Simon & Schuster, Inc.
All rights reserved, including the right of
reproduction in whole or in part in any form.
ALADDIN PAPERBACKS, NANCY DREW, and colophon are registered trademarks of Simon & Schuster, Inc.
NANCY DREW: GIRL DETECTIVE is a trademark of
Simon & Schuster, Inc.
First Aladdin Paperbacks edition March 2005
Printed in the United States of America
10 9 8 7 6 5 4 3 2 1
Library of Congress Control Number 2004108763
ISBN 0-689-86937-1

Contents

1	What's the Buzz?	1
2	Choosing Sides	11
3	Rude Surprise	25
4	Words in Haste	38
5	Open Season	49
6	No Stone Unturned	60
7	Rockets' Red Glare	70
8	Double Trouble	84
9	With Every Intent	92
10	Missing in Action	103
11	The Real Deal	116
12	No Stopping Now	127
13	Heat of Battle	136

Uncivil Acts

What's the Buzz?

Nancy, is that you?"

I heard my best friend Bess Marvin's voice behind me, fluttering above the crowd in one of our favorite River Heights hangouts, Susie's Read & Feed.

Across the table Bess's cousin George—who happens to be my *other* best friend—rolled her eyes. "Looks like Bess has gone shopping again."

Bess threaded through the restaurant, holding a big round hatbox above her head. "It finally got here!" Bess exclaimed. "I was so afraid it wouldn't arrive before the big day on Saturday."

"Bess went crazy online, ordering clothes from the eighteen sixties to wear to the Civil War reenactment on Saturday," George explained to me dryly. "The

1

only reason she ever goes online is to shop—and save money."

Bess plopped down the box, flipped off its lid, and plunged her hands deep into the tissue paper. "This bonnet is just too *perfect*, don't you think?" She lifted out a pale straw bonnet with a shallow crown, wide brim, and blue satin ribbons that perfectly matched her sparkling blue eyes. Slipping it on over her long blond curls, she tied the ribbons under her chin, fluffing them into a fat bow.

I had to admit, she did look adorable. But then, Bess always does. Of the three of us, she's the natural beauty. It helps, of course, that she actually pays attention to what she wears and how her hair is done. Most of the time George and I just can't be bothered.

"I also got this enormous hoop skirt, with layers and layers of petticoats to go over it," Bess continued. "And a gown of the most beautiful baby blue flowered dimity cotton. Come over to my house and I'll give you a fashion show!"

George's dark eyes flashed. "Gabriel Marvin is rolling over in his grave right now," she muttered.

"Who's Gabriel Marvin?" I asked. Bess yanked off her bonnet and slid into the chair we had waiting for her. "Gabriel Marvin was our great-great-great-great-grandfather," she explained. "My mom went to the city archives last week and got copies of some old records. As it turns out, he was the commanding officer of the River Heights Civil War regiment!"

I raised my eyebrows. "Wow, that's cool."

"What about your ancestors, Nancy?" Bess asked. "Have you investigated them yet?"

"Dad checked our family history and found the names of two guys, Caleb and Carson Drew," I said. "I filed a request with the clerk Tuesday, and I'm picking up the results this afternoon."

"Carson, like your dad?" George asked.

I nodded. "It's an old Drew family name. From what we can tell, they were the right age to fight in 1861, when the war broke out. But I don't know if they even joined the army."

"Of course they did. Everybody joined the army back then," Bess declared. "Just like everyone in town is fighting in the reenactment Saturday."

George tugged on a lock of her short dark hair—a nervous habit she has. "Fighting? I'll be on the battlefield, and so will Nancy. But last I heard, Bess, you were just joining the women's auxiliary."

Bess stuck out her tongue at her cousin. "The women's auxiliary plays an important role too. We run the field hospital, make cloth bandages, knit socks, and cook for the troops."

George perked up. "Cooking? I didn't know they were going to serve refreshments during the battle."

Bess scrunched up her nose. "Don't get excited. The organizers are making us cook authentic grub like what the troops really ate—salted beef and hardtack and cornmeal mush. Totally gross." She pretended to stick two fingers down her throat and made a gagging noise. "I can barely stand to be in the cooking tent."

"Then switch into the army," I suggested. "It'd be so much fun! The three of us can fight together."

"You're forgetting the whole point of the reenactment for Bess—the clothes," George teased.

I couldn't resist adding a little dig of my own. "People who work in mess tents and hospitals don't need to be decked out like a Southern belle, Bess."

Bess picked a cherry tomato out of George's half-eaten salad. "Why did you say a *Southern* belle? Girls from the North had fashion sense too."

George moved her salad away to protect it from Bess. "Calm down, Scarlett. Nancy knows you'd rather die than play a Confederate."

That struck me as a pretty weird thing to say. It was so off the wall, in fact, that I had no snappy comeback ready. And before I could think of one, we were interrupted.

"Ladies, ladies," said Harold Safer, stopping by our table on his way out of the café. Harold runs the gourmet cheese shop in River Heights, and he's something of a local character. He's a sweet guy, though, and we three always enjoy his company.

"You're just the people I'm looking for," Harold said. "Mrs. Mahoney roped me into organizing this little picnic to kick off the reenactment, Friday night at Bluff View Park."

George widened her eyes. "*Little* picnic? There are signs plastered all over town."

Harold sighed. "Well, the event just keeps on growing. But it's a lovely idea, to celebrate the reenactment with a picnic. Sort of like the picnic in *The Music Man*—do you know that musical, girls? I saw the most brilliant revival of it in New York!"

I held my breath. It's dangerous to let Harold Safer get on the subject of musicals. He could go on and on about them. I was annoyed when Bess gushed back, "Ooh, I've seen the movie. That one is a *classic*."

Harold smiled fondly. "Isn't it? Don't you just love the part where—"

Suddenly a bouncy, short woman with curly red hair barged up to us. She briskly stuck out a hand for Bess to shake. "Pam Mattei, Dawn's Early Light Productions. We're supplying the big pyrotechnical display for Friday night's picnic."

Now, something about this woman bugged me right away. Maybe it was her piercing gaze or her aggressive body language. Whatever it was, I had a gut feeling she was hiding something. Harold beamed. "Pamela

5

here suggested we distribute glow-in-the-dark necklaces before the fireworks. Could you youngsters help us with that?"

"Ooh, glow-in-the-dark necklaces, how fun!" Bess exclaimed. "The kids are going to love that!"

"E-mail me the details, George," I said, standing up. "I'd better get over to the archives. There may be a big crowd there, all looking up their ancestors before Saturday."

"I doubt it," George said with a shrug. "Most people have already searched their family trees on the Internet."

"Well, I'll go anyway," I said, feeling a little edgy. "See ya." I scooped up my bill, grabbed my purse and jacket off my chair, and left the table.

As I went to the cashier's desk to pay for my lunch, I wondered why I felt so peeved with Bess and George. It wasn't until I was outside in the fresh air that I finally figured it out.

I realized that I was feeling plain old jealous—jealous and left out. Bess and George have a full set of parents each, plus Bess has a little sister and George has two brothers. And as if that wasn't enough, they have each other, first cousins, living just a couple streets away.

Me? I'm an only child. My mom died when I was only three years old. My dad and I are real tight, sure,

6

but we have to be—we're the only immediate family either of us has.

I drew a deep breath. Now that I'd figured it out, I felt better. I'd overreacted, that was all. Bess and George didn't mean to make me feel bad. Usually they're supersensitive to my situation. It was just this Civil War history thing, making everyone focus on family more than usual. Now that I'd put it in perspective, I could deal with it.

"Nancy, wait up!" I heard Harold Safer call out behind me. He caught up and fell into step at my side. "Can you come to a picnic planning meeting tomorrow afternoon? Both Bess and George said they have other plans. It's at two P.M., at the historical society. It's all part of their seventy-fifth anniversary celebration, you know."

"Sure, I'll come to the meeting," I agreed.

"George said that you and she are playing the parts of soldiers in the battle on Saturday," he continued as we walked. "That sounds so thrilling! Which regiment will you be fighting with?"

"I don't know yet," I admitted. "That's why I'm going to the archives—to find out where my folks fought. I think it's a cool idea to sign up for the same regiment your ancestors were in."

"Oh, I couldn't agree with you more," Harold said. "Most people I've spoken with are doing that. An overwhelming number of them seem to be related to the Seventh Illinois Regiment, I've noticed. It was quite large, drew folks from miles away, even a few who lived outside Illinois."

"I guess that's not surprising when you think about it," I said. "It's basic math. Suppose a handful of veterans from that regiment settled in the states around here after the war. If they kept having children, and their children had children, and everybody stayed in or around River Heights—well, there would be a whole lot of them by now, all from the same few ancestors."

Harold chewed his lip. "But it still seems odd to me. If I remember local history, this area was settled by small farmers from both Southern and Northern states. Almost as many volunteered for the Confederate army as for the Union army. Sometimes even two brothers would go different ways—it tore whole families apart. I've always thought it was terribly sad, like one huge nationwide soap opera." He sighed dramatically. "Anyway, you'd figure that the descendants of those Confederate veterans would live around here, too. Yet no one I know has volunteered to join the Confederate army on Saturday."

"Really?" I thought for a second and realized I didn't know any Southern volunteers either. "How are they even going to hold a battle if the other side doesn't show up?"

"The organizers must have some plan," Harold said, always an optimist. He suddenly stopped walking. "Well, here's city hall. Good luck with your search."

"Thanks." With a brief good-bye, I headed up the steps.

The city archives are on the ground floor of city hall in a well-lit modern room. Since the original city hall washed away in a flood in the 1920s, the current one doesn't have a lot of dusty old file cabinets—just computer monitors and microfiche readers. To get any pre-1920s information, we have to give a request slip to a clerk. The clerk e-mails queries to local churches, schools, hospitals, and neighboring towns to piece together information from their files. Sometimes it takes days to get an answer.

My dad had found the names of our 1860s relatives in an old family Bible. If Caleb and Carson Drew had had any business dealings in the area, there was bound to be some record of them. And if they had joined a regiment—say, the Seventh Illinois, like so many other people in town—they should be in the government's files.

The records clerk who'd taken my request two days ealier smiled when she saw me. "Miss Drew? You're in luck." She pulled a manila folder from a tall stack on her desk.

I felt a buzz of excitement. "You found some trace of the Drew brothers?"

"More than a trace," she said. "We found baptism records from their church, enrollment lists from their school, land transactions in the county files. They signed the church wedding registries when they got married—Caleb in 1861, and his younger brother, Carson, in 1869, after the war. Oh, you can be proud of them. They were apparently well-respected local citizens."

A swell of pride rose in my chest. "What about their war records?" I flipped open the folder she'd handed me and glanced at the top sheet. As I read the sheet my heart began to hammer in my chest.

"Oh, they both did their duty all right," the clerk continued. "The government records show that Caleb was a sergeant, and Carson rose all the way to the rank of lieutenant—both in the Sixty-seventh Tennessee Regiment."

"Tennessee?" My voice came out in a croak.

"Yes indeed," she replied. "There were many Confederate sympathizers in town, you know. And when the war started, they all went down to the Southern states to join up."

Which meant . . . Caleb and Carson Drew had been Johnny Rebs!

2

Choosing Sides

I just kept staring at that piece of paper. It made me feel queasy. It was so different from what I'd expected. George and Bess had been my best friends my whole life. I guess I'd just assumed that, six generations ago, the Drew brothers had fought arm in arm with Gabriel Marvin. Was I wrong!

My instincts told me to keep this news quiet. Normally I don't hide anything from my two best buds, but I wasn't sure how they'd react to this. I'd been set on the idea of joining the same regiment as the Drews. I believe in being true to the facts, and the fact was, the Drews had followed the Southern cause. But would Bess and George want me to turn my back on that?

I walked out of city hall lost in thought. I didn't

notice the doors swinging shut behind me. A man coming up the steps lunged, trying to catch the heavy door before it closed. "Hey, kid!" he shouted rudely.

I blinked and looked at him. He was middle aged, burly, and balding, wearing a loud tweed sports jacket. "Sorry," I murmured.

He peered at me. "Wait, you're Carson Drew's daughter, aren't you?"

I nodded cautiously. Most people in town think my dad, Carson Drew, is the best lawyer around, and I won't argue with that. Still, if you win enough cases, you're bound to cross some people. I'd had enough run-ins with people who held a grudge against my dad—I'd learned to be careful.

"I'm Arthur Jeffries," the man said, scowling. I gave him a blank look. "Jeffries Autorama?" he added.

"Oh, right!" I recalled a huge used-car lot out on State Avenue, bedecked with big signs and shiny pennants and speakers blaring loud music.

He rocked back on his heels. "I guess you know I'm running the Union army in our battle Saturday."

I nodded as if I did. But really, I hadn't a clue before he told me.

"We've got a bunch of these reenactors coming to town," Jeffries said, "and I'm too busy to show them around. Your dad said I could ask him for help. I guess that means I can call on you, too."

He motioned to the other man behind him, a younger man with longish dark hair and a really impressive mustache. The second man grinned and gave me a little wave. I liked him right away.

"This here's Todd Willetts," Jeffries said. "He's the captain of—what was it, Todd?"

"Eighth New York Volunteers," Willetts said.

"Whatever." Jeffries began to sidle inside city hall, his mind already on his next errand. "Miss Drew will show you to the bazaar, Willetts. I'll see you there later." He hustled into the building.

Willetts rolled his eyes. "Big cheese," he joked. "Please, don't let me impose on you. If you'll just point me to Sixth and River Street—"

"I'm happy to take you there," I offered. I figured it would help me get my mind off the news I'd just received. "I heard they'd set up a Civil War bazaar in the old anvil warehouse. I've been wanting to check it out."

Todd Willetts turned out to be easy to talk to, and I ended up enjoying the five-block walk to the bazaar with him. "What's your regiment again?" I asked as we walked along.

"Eighth New York Volunteers," Willetts said. I thought I heard a bit of a Southern drawl as he spoke. "We're just a club of Civil War nuts who like to dress up and play war. We model ourselves after a real Civil War company, though. We started out joining in reenactments of any battle the original Eighth New York fought in. But now, shoot, we have so much fun, some of us show up at any reenactment we can find—like this one. The Eighth New York wasn't at your battle at all. But since our guys know how to do things authentically, and this is the first time this battle's been done, we offered to come help."

"So you're from New York?"

"Not me—I live in Kentucky. Lots of the guys live around upstate New York, but there's no rule. Some folks joined just because we have a reputation as an active bunch, with cool uniforms."

"So if I wanted to fight in this battle, I could pick whatever side I wanted?" I asked hopefully. Maybe I could hang out with Bess and George after all.

"Sure," he said. "Guys whose families immigrated to America after the war, for example, pick any regiment they like. But I do believe in honoring your own family. My ancestor was in the original Eighth New York. That's why I travel so far to take up arms with them."

I stifled a sigh. In my heart I had to admit I felt the same way.

Soon we reached River Street. This part of town had been pretty run down in past years, but new shops and renovations had turned things around. The side wall of the massive redbrick warehouse before us was painted with faded letters: MAHONEY ANVIL COMPANY.

"Mahoney, eh?" Todd said. "Isn't that the lady who runs the historical society? I remember it from the letters she wrote us."

"Yes, Mrs. Mahoney is a big supporter of this reenactment," I said. "It's all planned to celebrate the historical society's seventy-fifth anniversary. And since her husband's family owned the anvil business—they used to be the biggest employers in River Heights— she lent this empty warehouse to the town for the Civil War vendors."

I'd always wondered what the warehouse looked like inside. We entered a cavernous space, its crumbling brick walls pierced by a few tiny, dust-coated windows. The entire floor was filled with temporary booths, framed in steel pipes with canvas walls. Each vendor had hung a sign and set up tables of their wares. River Heights citizens shuffled through the aisles, gaping at the unusual items—some valuable antiques, and others clever reproductions, all with some connection to the 1860s and the Civil War.

I was astonished by the variety of things for sale: Confederate money, antique belt buckles and buttons, vintage chess sets and decks of cards, canteens and cutlery, boots, blankets, and backpacks. One dealer specialized in the blue uniforms of the North, another in the gray uniforms of the South. But by far the greatest number of booths displayed weapons—everything from knives small enough to hide in your boot to big lumbering cannons mounted on wheels.

"This is like a window into another time," I said, wide eyed.

"Sure is, Nancy," said a familiar voice behind me. I turned around to see our housekeeper, Hannah Gruen, inspecting the carved hilt of a long saber. "I can just imagine my great-great-uncle Adolph Gruen here."

"Did he fight in the Civil War?" I asked.

Hannah shook her head and laughed. "Goodness no, Nancy. He didn't care about North or South—he had just moved here from Germany. But he was a smart shopkeeper who smelled a good business opportunity. He made a very nice profit during the war, selling guns to both sides."

"Guns from Germany?" Todd asked, leaning over my shoulder. "Those were so heavy, some soldiers could barely lift them. Besides, they were muskets. The real guns to have were rifles, which had grooves inside the barrels to make them shoot straighter. And toward the end of the war, gunmakers came out with the first repeating rifles—soldiers could fire six shots without having to stop and reload."

Hannah opened her eyes wide. "Nancy, you have a history professor here!"

Todd laughed. "No, ma'am, just a Civil War buff. I'm Todd Willetts, one of the reenactors. We show up like locusts whenever a good town like yours puts together one of these pretend battles."

Hannah shook Todd's hand and promptly gave him an open invitation to the Drew home for dinner. That was just like Hannah. She's so warm and generous, she wants to feed the world. She has more or less raised me since my mom died, and I couldn't love her more.

As we browsed around the bazaar, I noticed that Todd greeted several vendors by name. "You all know one another?" I remarked.

Todd nodded sheepishly. "It's a small world. Whenever there's a reenactment, we show up, and so do these sutlers. That was the term, back then, used to describe traveling salesmen."

I looked down and realized that I was idly sifting through a bin of smooth, heavy metal objects—bullets. I pulled my hand back, feeling a shiver. As a detective, I've had dealings with guns, and I don't like them. Guns always turn things ugly.

Todd frowned. "Why is this guy selling bullets? No one uses bullets in a reenactment—that's one of the ground rules. Soldiers fire blanks at one another

17

and then fall down and pretend to be dead, or wounded. No one really gets hurt." He looked up at the sign hung on the booth. "Emory's Armory. I should have known."

I couldn't let that remark pass. "Emory? Who's he?"

Willetts shrugged. "I shouldn't have said that. I don't know anything against Nathan for certain."

He wasn't going to get away from me that easily. "What is it?" I cued him.

Todd sighed. "You can't believe everything you hear. This is a pretty tight business, and dealers will trash their competitors. But Emory . . . well, not everything he sells is what he says it is. He'll tell you something is an antique when it's just a reproduction, or he'll say it's a copy of the model of gun you want when it isn't. Reenactors like to be authentic. So when an expert like Emory tells us the wrong stuff and we believe it, we get burned."

I turned to get a look at Nathan Emory. I spotted a fortyish man, medium height, brown hair, plaid shirt and khakis—so ordinary, you'd never pick him out of a lineup. He sure was putting the press on his customer—who happened to be Arthur Jeffries.

"Actually, it is a reproduction, but made by a real craftsman," Emory was saying. "Look at the wood on that gunstock—beautiful, eh? There never was a finer gun than the Springfield rifle."

I saw Jeffries take the gun in his hands and heft it, testing the weight. "How much?" he asked.

"List price is four hundred. I can let you have it for three seventy-five," Emory said. "But you'll have to decide quick. I haven't got too many left."

Jeffries's eyes sparkled, as if he couldn't resist nabbing a rare model. He fished a credit card out of his pocket. "You take plastic?"

"Sure do," Emory said, and he rang up the sale. "And here are the forms for you to fill out to get your gun permit. Remember, there's a twenty-four-hour waiting period before the permit becomes effective. That gives the state time to run a computer check to make sure you're responsible. We don't want guns falling into the wrong hands."

As I began to back away from Emory's booth, I felt myself grabbed from behind. I whirled around to see my father. "Hey, Nancy, why so jumpy? I was just going to give you a kiss," Dad said, leaning over and laying a quick smooch on my cheek.

"Oh, I don't know, Dad. Being around all these weapons makes me nervous," I admitted.

"Just think of them as stage props," my dad said. "This reenactment is a big play, that's all."

I told him what I had learned about the Drew brothers. He nodded. "I know. I called the archives myself, earlier today. Based on what I learned, I signed up with the Sixty-seventh Tennessee Regiment. And now, to play my part, I'll need a gun. This fellow has a big inventory." He pointed to Emory's Armory. "And if it's good enough for Art Jeffries, it's good enough for me." He watched the car dealer strut away with his new gun.

"Dad, I'm not sure—," I began. I looked around for Todd, but he seemed to have disappeared. I hated to repeat gossip about the dealer, but I didn't want my dad swindled.

"That looked like a fine gun Art bought," Dad was saying to Nathan Emory. "Can I see that model?"

Nathan Emory paused, studying my dad. "What regiment are you fighting with?" he asked.

"The Tennessee regulars," Dad reported.

Was it my imagination, or did Nathan Emory's face tighten up? "I guess you could carry a Springfield, then," he said coolly. "Four hundred fifty dollars—take it or leave it."

I elbowed in front of my dad. "But you just sold that same gun to Mr. Jeffries for three hundred seventy-five," I protested.

Nathan Emory looked at me, flushing. "Well, uh, of course, but—he'd earned a special discount. Besides," Emory rushed on, "you wouldn't buy *exactly* the same gun. I'd sell you a version more like the South used—a .577 caliber British Enfield rifle. Of course, if you object, I could always come down in price . . ."

I felt my blood boil. It wasn't that I didn't want my dad getting a deal—I didn't want him to buy anything at all from such a shifty trader. I was relieved when Dad shook his head and walked away from the booth. But I couldn't miss the glare Nathan Emory gave me before he turned away.

Dad and I had gone only a few steps up the aisle before Art Jeffries stopped us. "Carson," he said in this bossy tone. "I need your help. All of our local hotels are booked solid, you see, and—"

"That's great news, Art," Dad remarked. "You were right when you said this reenactment would be good for local businesses."

Art Jeffries looked smug. "No question about that. But now we've got a lot of out-of-towners with no place to stay. And we need them to fill out the Confederate numbers, since most River Heights folks have gone Union. You've got a big house. Suppose you could put up a few rebs for a night or two?"

"Wouldn't mind at all," Dad said. "Especially being a reb myself."

Jeffries looked shocked. "You—you are? Well, uh, okay. I'll tell Lisa Mandell, the South's housing coordinator." Lowering his head, he rushed away like he was glad to be rid of us.

What was up with that?

"Mr. Drew, good for you," a girl's voice purred behind us. I knew at once it was Deirdre Shannon. I've known her all my life, but we've never really been friends. For some reason she always seems to try to beat me at everything I do. I suppose you could say she's my rival—that is, if I actually *cared* about beating her. Why bother?

"I'm glad to hear somebody has enough integrity to fight for the South," Deirdre went on. Deirdre, talking about integrity? Now *there's* a laugh!

"Don't tell me you are too," I said.

"Of course," she shot back. "My great-great-great-great-grandfather was a reb, and I'm going to be one too. One thing, though, Nancy."

I glared at her. "What's that?"

"As you know," she half-drawled, "some Confederate soldiers had gray uniforms. Others had to use cloth that was home-dyed with butternut juice. Now, with that strawberry blond hair of yours, Nancy, butternut brown would look awful. But I think butternut would be fabulous with my hair. Which color uniform are you going to rent?"

I tried to act casual. "I haven't decided yet. In fact, I haven't decided whether I'm fighting for North or South, DeeDee." I knew that using her old childhood nickname would annoy her—it always does.

Deirdre seethed and stomped away.

22

"You haven't decided yet? Why is that, Nancy?" Dad said, sounding hurt. "Now that we know the Drew brothers fought for the South—"

"I know, Dad," I interrupted. "But Bess and George and I want to fight together. After all, the North wanted to end slavery, and ending slavery was a good thing."

Dad shrugged. "Well, slavery wasn't the only issue. Even in the Union army, nine out of ten soldiers didn't care about slavery. And as far as the Southerners went, they didn't fight *for* slavery—they fought for the right to make their own laws, without federal interference."

"I never read that," I said weakly. I should know better than to argue with my dad. He *is* the best lawyer in River Heights, after all.

"Mr. Drew?" Dad turned to face a slightly large older man with curly, steel gray hair. The man pushed his glasses up the bridge of his nose. "I'm Marcus Hammond. Ms. Mandell told me you might have a room to rent."

"No rent needed. Be our guest," Dad offered, shaking Hammond's hand. "Welcome to River Heights."

Hammond blinked. "Oh, I've been here before. Used to live here, in fact—twenty-five years ago." He smiled shyly. "The town's changed a lot."

"Sure has," Dad agreed. "Welcome home, then."

Dad introduced Hammond to me and began giving him directions to our home. Just then I spied Todd Willetts down the aisle. I waved to him. "Dad, there's a reenactor I met earlier. Let's tell him about that guy switching gun prices on you."

Dad and Hammond both looked over at Todd Willetts. Hammond abruptly snatched up his duffle bag. "Er, I'll find the house, no problem," he said, backing away. "See you there. Got to run." And he melted into the crowd like a puff of smoke.

"Huh," Dad said, staring after him. "Funny guy. So who's this friend of yours, Nancy?"

Todd had just walked up to us. "How do you know Martin Halstead?" he asked me.

I frowned. "Martin Halstead? Never heard of him. That man's name was Hammond—Marcus Hammond."

Willetts shook his head. "I don't care what name he gave you. That's Martin Halstead, all right."

3

Rude Surprise

I was still brooding about Todd Willett's remark that evening as I took a seat at the meeting of the River Heights Historical Society. It was in this big old Victorian house on River Street that the society had taken over and made into a museum. A group of older ladies seem to spend most of their time there, putting up displays and arguing over the details of our town's past.

From the size of the gathering crowd, it seemed like practically everyone in town was going to show up. Seemed like the reenactment had finally gotten people excited about River Heights history.

"This reenactment has been a great way for the historical society to celebrate its seventy-fifth anniversary," I said to my boyfriend, Ned Nickerson, who was sitting next to me. You might think a historical society meeting is no place for an exciting date, but it is when you're going out with a college student who loves history.

"I bet Mrs. Mahoney's thrilled," I added. Agnes Mahoney, the president of the society, is known for her involvement with local charities and civic projects.

Ned grinned that great lopsided grin of his. He has brown hair and brown eyes and killer dimples—and the best thing about him is that he doesn't even know what a hunk he is. "A minute ago she looked upset that folks were trampling that Turkish rug in the front parlor," he said. "But she'll get over it. She loves being the center of attention, and tonight she's it."

Just then I spotted a thick braid of salt-and-pepper hair two rows ahead of us. The braid was unmistakable; it belonged to Evaline Waters, head librarian at the River Heights Public Library all the years I was growing up. I couldn't tell you how many rainy Saturdays I spent poking around the library shelves with her when I was a kid. She's retired now, but I still visit her every couple of weeks or so.

I leaned forward to get her attention. I saw Ms. Waters's face light up as she greeted a friend, with even more sunniness than usual. I glanced over to see whom she was meeting.

Marcus Hammond!

He'd been so present in my mind, I just stiffened with shock. "Mr. Hammond and Ms. Waters know each other?" I whispered to Ned.

"You mean your new lodger?" Ned asked. "Well, you said he once lived here—it's natural he'd have some old friends." He leaned forward. "Hi, Ms. Waters."

Twisting around in her seat, Ms. Waters caught sight of us and smiled. But Mr. Hammond's expression was very different. Was his scowl permanent, or was it just us?

"Glad to see you here, Mr. Hammond," I called out. "It must be fun to reconnect with River Heights after all these years. Where do you live now, by the way?" Sure, it sounded pushy, but sometimes, direct questions are the best way to get to the bottom of things.

He looked annoyed, but I got an answer. "Potsdam, New York. But only for a year or so."

I nodded. "Do you know a man there named Martin Halstead?"

I'm telling you, he was good. He barely showed any reaction! But a flicker deep in his eyes told me I'd struck pay dirt. "Martin Halstead?" he repeated. "I don't recall anyone by that name. But then, I haven't lived there long. As I was saying, Evaline," he went on, making a big point of turning back and lowering his voice to continue their private conversation.

Clearly Hammond was using Ms. Waters like a shield to prevent me from asking more questions. But if he thought that would work, he didn't know Nancy Drew. "The thing is, Mr. Hammond," I said, raising my voice, "at the bazaar this afternoon, a friend of mine saw you and he *swore* you were a guy he knew named Martin Halstead."

"Well, he must have me confused with someone else!" Hammond snapped over his shoulder. "Someone who happens to look like me maybe."

"My friend's name is Todd Willetts. Sound familiar?" I pressed on. Ned, embarrassed, gave me a warning nudge with his knee, but I ignored him.

"Never heard of him," Hammond replied, turning his back on me again.

"Guess I'm not scoring points with Ms. Waters's old boyfriend," I muttered to Ned.

"Old boyfriend? What makes you say that?"

Really, guys can be so clueless. "Come on, Ned, watch their body language," I said. "See how they lean toward each other? See how she tilts her head down to give him that upward gaze with all the eyelashes working? Classic flirting behavior."

Ned looked puzzled. "But they must be in their sixties!"

Now it was my turn to smack his knee. "So what?

People don't stop liking each other after they turn thirty! You know, I've always wondered why Ms. Waters never married. Maybe Marcus Hammond was her long-lost love."

"That's romantic mush. You've been hanging around Bess too much," Ned teased me.

That was a sore point. "No, actually, I haven't," I admitted. "I've, uh, been avoiding her. I'm not sure how she'll take the news about the Drew brothers being Confederates."

"Why should she care?" Ned asked.

"Because she and George are all worked up about being related to the Union hero Gabriel Marvin, that's why," I said. I tried not to sound bitter, but the way Ned crooked one eyebrow told me I hadn't succeeded.

"Don't get me involved, Nancy," Ned said, raising his hands in surrender. "I refuse to take sides."

"Why? What about your ancestors, Ned?"

"They were Quakers," Ned said proudly, "the original pacifists. They were totally against war, any war. And I plan to follow their example."

"You're just weaseling out of the argument," I teased him. Still, I felt frustrated. I wouldn't have Ned's partnership on the battlefield.

"So you've made up your mind to fight as a Southerner?" he asked.

"Oh, it's all just playacting," I said, repeating what my dad had said that afternoon. "Somebody has to show up to play the Confederates—it might as well be me. It's like a part in a mystery play—someone has to play the murderer, someone gets to be the detective."

"And someone else has to play the victim, and lie like a corpse midstage for most of the play," Ned added with a grin.

"Order, please. Order!" the reedy voice of Agnes Mahoney quavered into a microphone. The excited crowd gradually fell silent. Once the room was quiet, Mrs. Mahoney, looking elegant in a peach-colored wool suit, launched into a speech about the role of River Heights in the Civil War. I'd caught bits and pieces of the story over the last few weeks, but the whole tale was fascinating.

Like all the old towns in our part of the country, River Heights is pretty far from where most of the Civil War fighting took place. Still, when war broke out in 1861, the local men, all excited, began to meet for drilling and target practice. There were maybe a hundred men at first. But as weeks went by and news trickled in, they began to argue politics. It became clear that their "company" couldn't even agree on which side of the war to fight for.

Finally they split in two. Fifty or sixty men marched off to join the Seventh Illinois Regiment of the Union army. About a dozen others went to join a Michigan regiment. But a band of thirty or forty soldiers straggled several miles to offer their services to the Confederate States of America. And in 1864, by coincidence, all three regiments showed up in West Virginia at the Battle of Black Creek.

"I first knew of Black Creek because of my late husband's forefather Josiah Mahoney," Mrs. Mahoney continued. "Their family had always treasured the medal he won for his bravery there. Josiah was a raw young man of twenty-six when he joined up with the Seventh Illinois—"

"Josiah Mahoney never enlisted in the Seventh Illinois Regiment," a clear voice rang out. The crowd gasped.

In front of us Evaline Waters stood up, waving a handful of papers. "There is no record of his enlistment," she announced. "I have here, however, a photocopy of his enlistment papers—in the Sixty-ninth New York Regiment."

A wave of murmurs washed over the room.

"The Sixty-ninth New York Regiment was made up of poor Irish immigrants," she went on. Everyone was listening so hard, you could have heard a pin drop. "They'd just stepped off the boat in New York Harbor. They had no jobs or places to live, so they joined the army. They were promised American citizenship if they'd fight for the Union. And as the war went on, the Sixty-ninth New York was distinguished by one statistic—the highest desertion rate in the Union army."

Evaline swallowed and went on, her voice beginning to tremble. "They were part of the Union forces at Black Creek, all right. But Josiah Mahoney wasn't going to fight with them. The night before the battle, he skipped camp. A few fellows from the Seventh Illinois caught him stealing bacon before dawn the next morning. They stuck a gun in his hands and forced him to fight with them."

Mrs. Mahoney gripped the edge of her lectern. I was afraid she was going to faint. "But the medal—," she began faintly.

"The medal may be real," Evaline Waters said. "But there's no record of one ever being awarded to Josiah Mahoney. Maybe he picked it off a dead soldier in battle." The crowd gasped again.

"It is true," Ms. Waters said, "that he was wounded in the leg at Black Creek and discharged. But I have here a letter from an army surgeon who claims Josiah cut himself in the leg to get out of having to fight anymore. He marched back to River Heights with other wounded men, all right—because he was afraid to go back to his own troop. He settled down here, and the rest is history."

As Ms. Waters sat down a flood of excited whispers rose. "Why would Ms. Waters dig up such information, and then make it public here?" I whispered to Ned. "She had to know it would embarrass Mrs. Mahoney."

Ned looked stumped. "Stirring up trouble like that isn't Ms. Waters's style at all," he agreed.

Mrs. Mahoney raised her voice over the crowd's murmurs. I could hear the angry voice of Arthur Jeffries in particular. "However that may be," Mrs. Mahoney insisted, trying to cover her embarrassment by moving on to a new topic, "we all agree that the real hero of the River Heights troop was their leader, Colonel Gabriel Marvin."

I glanced over at Bess and George, standing by a side wall. Bess had a big grin plastered on her face. So did George.

As Mrs. Mahoney went on, I realized that this Colonel Marvin really was some big deal. Bess had every right to be proud of being related to the guy. But did she have to show it off so much?

The minute the lecture was over, people popped out of their seats and gathered in buzzing clusters. It wasn't every day you saw a Mahoney getting shown up. I hopped over the row in front of me to get to Evaline Waters. "Wow, Ms. Waters, how did you find out all of that stuff about Josiah Mahoney?"

Ms. Waters looked flushed and confused. "Oh, I just did some online research. It's amazing what you can find online. Right, Marcus? My friend Marcus here showed me how to do it. As you may know, he runs his own historical Web site—www.yourhistory.com."

I raised my eyebrows. "Really? The Web site everybody in town used to trace their genealogy?" I had to admit, that impressed me.

Marcus Hammond crossed his arms tightly and looked down, as if the attention made him uneasy. "Evaline did a lot of the research. I just showed her where to look."

Now it made sense. Revealing the truth about Josiah Mahoney was a perfect advertisement for YourHistory.com. Ms. Waters was doing her old friend a favor. But was it worth shaming Mrs. Mahoney for that? And what made Marcus Hammond start digging around Mahoney family history in the first place?

With so many people crowding around Ms. Waters, I was soon pushed aside. I scanned the crowd and found Ned talking to Bess and George. I figured it was as good a time as any to spring my news on them.

As I got closer, I heard Bess saying, "Well, we always knew the Marvins had been leaders. They had their own village, Marvinville, before the town was incorporated. Gabriel Marvin was promoted all the way to

34

major in just a few months! The Seventh Illinois was a very strong regiment—we won most of our battles."

"Sure, but it's easier when you're equipped with Henry rifles." Todd Willetts stepped forward and broke in. "Lots of Illinois regiments had big Chicago money bankrolling them—fighting against ragtag Tennessee and Virginia kids with old shotguns and squirrel guns in their hands. By that point in the war, it was more about financing than military skill."

Bess stared at Todd, two red spots burning in her cheeks. "Bravery is bravery," she insisted.

"I'm not saying your ancestor wasn't brave," Todd allowed. "But Black Creek was especially unequal. Not in numbers—there were just as many soldiers on both sides—but in equipment. It's a wonder that the Confederates did so well. That's where true bravery comes in."

George laid her hands on Bess's shoulder. "Me, I've decided not to play Gabriel Marvin after all," she began. Typical George—trying to change the subject to get her cousin out of hot water. "I did research and found another historical person, Callie McGee. She dressed as a boy so she could fight alongside her brothers in the Twelfth Michigan Regiment. Talk about brave!"

But nobody was listening to George. "Nancy, tell your friend he's out of line," Bess ordered me.

"I'm sorry, Bess, but I actually wouldn't argue history with Todd," I said. "He knows this stuff backwards and forwards. He's an experienced reenactor, with the Eighth New York Volunteers."

Bess tossed her head. "He wears a Union uniform—and he's talking like that?"

Todd shrugged. "I won't be wearing Union blue on Saturday. I've agreed to act in a Confederate regiment because so few people signed up for them."

"Like Todd says," I butted in, "the numbers of soldiers on each side were even at Black Creek. But I've heard that, so far, River Heights has seven hundred people signed up for the North—and only sixty-eight for the South. The reenactment won't work if we don't get the numbers balanced."

I should have known better than to cross Bess in front of a cute guy like Todd. It was only later that I realized I had shamed her—kind of like Evaline Waters had just shamed Mrs. Mahoney.

Hands clenched at her sides, Bess gave me a deadly glare. "Is it true, Nancy Drew? Is it true what Deirdre told me—that you're going to turn traitor and fight for the South?"

My face was burning too. "So what if I do? It's just a big play. And the Drew brothers believed—"

Bess groaned. "Forget the Drew brothers, Nancy! The North stood for freedom—the South stood for slavery. If you can't stand up for what's right . . ."

I wish I could've remembered the history stuff my dad had explained to me. But I was so furious, I had to let it get personal. "Who are you to tell me which side to take?" I spluttered. I turned to George. "George, would you please talk some sense into your cousin?"

George squirmed. She looked over at her cousin. Bess practically had steam blowing out of her ears, she was so mad.

"Sorry, Nan," George said slowly. "But I . . . I've got to side with Bess on this one."

4

Words in Haste

Okay, **I'll admit it**, I lost my temper. I probably could have said something sweet and soothing right then to get back in with Bess and George. But I just couldn't make myself do it. All I could come up with was, "Well, Bess, if that's how you feel—"

"Yes, that's how I feel," Bess shot back. You know, she can be as stubborn as me sometimes.

I shrugged like I didn't care. I knew it would make her even madder, but I couldn't help it. "Then I guess I'll go ahead and sign up for the Confederate army," I said. "If you're going to be mad at me anyway...."

"Oh, come on, Nancy—," George started, but Bess cut her off.

"No, George, let her go do what she wants," Bess

said. She whirled around and stalked away, blue eyes blazing. And I guess mine were too!

That was that. I crossed the room to the sign-up desk and put my name down to join the Confederate army.

I slept later than usual the next morning. I'd been tossing and turning all night, feeling rotten about that fight with Bess. By the time I got up, I had only one thing on my mind: calling Bess and getting the whole dumb argument settled. I picked up my bedside phone and punched the speed-dial button for the Marvins.

Bess's little sister, Maggie, answered. She recognized my voice right away. "Ooh, Nancy, what did you do? Bess said if you called, I was supposed to say she's out."

"Come on, Maggie, let me talk to her."

"I can't."

"Why not?"

"Because she really isn't here."

"Okay." Maggie can be such a brat sometimes. "Then I'll call back later."

"Good lu-uck," Maggie replied in a singsong voice, and hung up.

I blew out a sigh of total exasperation. Bess was

taking this battle thing way too far. I speed-dialed George. "Fayne residence," a kid's voice answered. That was Scott, George's pesky younger brother. "Hi, Scott, it's Nancy. Put George on?"

"Sure thing." Scott threw down the phone with a clatter and yelled *"Georgiaaaaaa!"* at the top of his lungs. Scott loves to tease his sister by calling her by her real first name.

I heard voices go back and forth, then clomping footsteps. "Just say I'll call her back," I heard George tell Scott in the background.

"You tell her yourself," Scott shot back.

There was a dull clatter as George picked up the phone. "Nancy, I can't talk right now, okay?" George pleaded, and disconnected the line.

I just sat there in shock. George had hung up on me! It was one thing to have Bess be in a snit, but George, too? Anything could bounce off that girl!

I pulled on some jeans and a T-shirt and went down to the kitchen. I wasn't just hungry for breakfast—I wanted Hannah's advice.

In the kitchen I found Hannah humming to herself, moving back and forth between the stove and the sink. "Morning, dear," she called out. "Pancakes?"

"Mmm, yes please," I said gratefully.

"I already have the batter mixed up. That lovely Mr. Hammond had a big stack earlier," Hannah reported, beaming. Nothing makes her happier than feeding someone with a good appetite. "Such a charming man. So polite!"

I'd forgotten about Marcus Hammond staying with us. Last night when I came home, I was so steamed up about Bess and George, I'd walked right by the guest bedroom door and didn't notice it was closed. "Oh, yeah, Mr. Hammond. Is he around?" I remembered now that there were things I wanted to ask him about—like why he'd changed his name, for starters.

"No. He said he had a million things to do around town," Hannah replied, waving her spatula in the air. "Your dad and he went to rent uniforms for the battle on Saturday."

Just thinking of the battle made me wince. "I signed up last night," I said, plopping down on a seat in our breakfast nook. "But I might change sides."

Hannah looked concerned. "Why?"

"Bess and George wanted me to fight with the Union troops instead," I explained.

Hannah set her hands on her hips. "So? Since when do you do only what they say? You girls have always let one another be independent."

"Usually," I said, fiddling with a fork. "But Bess got worked up about it. She said some hotheaded things last night . . . and so did I."

41

Hannah turned back to flip the sizzling pancakes. "I heard it was a spirited meeting, all right. But I'm sure when everybody's cooled down——"

"I called Bess this morning to apologize," I burst out. "She told Maggie to say she was out. And George hung up on me!"

Hannah stepped over to lay a hand on my hair. "Don't get too upset, Nancy," she said gently. "Give Bess some room, and she'll come around. If you treat it like a big deal, it'll turn into a big deal. You don't want that."

"I was willing to apologize—even though she was wrong and I wasn't!" I argued.

"Forget apologies," Hannah said with a shrug. "Stop worrying about who's wrong and who's right. Act like nothing happened, and then Bess will too."

"But what about George——"

"Don't hold it against George if she sides with her family. She has to do that," Hannah said, hurrying back to the stove. "Oops. Hope you don't mind if some of these got a little brown."

Hannah's advice lifted a weight off my shoulders. I actually felt upbeat by the time I got in my hybrid car and drove downtown.

My first stop that morning was the temporary office where the organizers of the Confederate army had set up headquarters. There was a short line out the front door. People coming out were carrying wads of clothing in plastic bags.

Just my luck—Deirdre Shannon was standing two people ahead of me in line. "Butternut or gray, Nancy?" she called, almost mocking me.

"Gray, I guess," I said.

"Some of those gray uniforms have a red stripe down the leg," Deirdre rattled on. "Very slimming. Ooh, and I saw somebody else had a jacket that had black cuffs with the most *beautiful* braid embroidery. I hope I get one of those!"

"The uniforms they rent out here are pretty basic," the man in front of me told her, sounding as irritated by Deirdre as I was getting. "They give you a long gray jacket with a stand-up collar, a leather belt to go over it, and gray pants. If you want something special, you'll have to buy it at the bazaar."

Deirdre didn't pick up on the man's scornful tone. "What are the hats like? I hope they're slouch hats, with a brim, not those dumb flat-topped caps."

"A kepi. They're called kepis," the man said.

Deirdre shrugged. "Whatever. They'd mash down my hair. Yuck."

Turning to get away from Deirdre, I was glad to see someone else I knew coming up the street—Charlie Adams. Charlie drives a tow truck for a local garage, and I've gotten to know him well. Maybe too well. My hybrid car goes so long between fill-ups, I have to admit I don't always remember to check the fuel gauge. Charlie's such a sweetheart, he never charges me for a tow anymore. Bess says it's because he has a crush on me. No comment!

"Charlie, are you joining up?" I asked.

Charlie shook his head. "No, I'm driving an earthmover," he said, stopping to chat.

I couldn't figure that out. "An earthmover? They had those in the Civil War?"

"Oh, I'm not driving one *during* the battle," Charlie explained. "*Before* the battle. I'm on landscape detail. We're taking Riverside Park and making it look like the land around Black Creek, where the battle was actually fought. We're rerouting a stream, building up a couple of ridges where the cannons were placed, and scooping out a hollow where there was some fierce hand-to-hand combat." He grinned. "We're even making huge papier-mâché boulders for sharpshooters to hide behind."

"Oh, yeah, I read about that in the paper," I said. "The committee hired a Civil War historian to research it and make it as authentic as possible."

By this time the line had moved up to the front door, so I waved good-bye to Charlie and stepped inside the office. Once my eyes got used to the light, I was surprised to see Nathan Emory, the gun dealer, with a stack of rifles at a card table next to the uniform desk. And who was talking to him but Pam Mattei, the red-haired fireworks exec who had been with Harold Safer yesterday. She was leaning over the table, talking behind her hand to Emory. Her eyes scanned the crowd as she talked. I felt a prickle along my skin—a sure sign that something was awry.

"Good idea, letting folks buy weapons at the same time," the man in front of me said to his neighbor. "Saves us a trip to the sutlers' bazaar."

"Yeah, but I wonder why that dealer got the exclusive rights," I said. Then an image flashed in my mind: Nathan Emory handing a rifle to Art Jeffries. Jeffries earned that discount all right. This was Nathan Emory's payoff . . . and a pretty sweet payoff it was!

As if reading my mind, Art Jeffries suddenly marched in the door, acting all official. "Just checking out things in the enemy camp," he joked in his booming voice.

Mrs. Mahoney, who'd been going over papers with one of the organizers, looked up. "Art," she said sweetly, "how handy that you're here. Before the picnic meeting this afternoon, I need someone to run an errand for me—"

Art Jeffries snorted. "Do I look like a gofer?"

Mrs. Mahoney studied him, puzzled. "What?"

45

"I've got plenty of my own things to take care of," Jeffries said. "You can't order me to run your errands."

Mrs. Mahoney drew her slender, frail figure up to its full height. I had to hand it to her, she had a lot of dignity. "But as president of the historical society—"

"Tell it to Josiah Mahoney. That is, if he hasn't run away yet," Jeffries sneered.

What was getting into everybody in River Heights? Was it just the reenactment turning them against one another? If things went on like this, pretty soon we'd have another war on our hands!

"You've gotten used to running everything in this town, lady," Jeffries told Mrs. Mahoney, getting more belligerent by the second. "Well, here's one thing you can't run. My guys and I have put a lot of effort into this battle already, and we aren't taking orders from the likes of you."

"But . . . the whole idea of the reenactment was mine in the first place!" Mrs. Mahoney spluttered.

"Tough luck," Jeffries shot back. "You can mess around with your little picnic all you want, but leave the battle plans to us menfolk." He leaned over, breathing hotly in her face. *Or else.*

I just plain didn't like Art Jeffries. I didn't like his manner. The thought of him kept running through my head that afternoon, as my mind drifted off during the meeting for Friday night's picnic. It was one of those meetings that seem like they'll never end.

I wished George and Bess were there. What kinds of things did they have going on instead? They probably smelled how boring this would be from home!

Pam Mattei was droning on. "So our rockets will be set up on a barge, tethered to the river bank. But what about power for the ignition devices?"

Harold Safer looked confused. "The designer at your headquarters told me you'd have a small generator right there on the barge."

Pam looked down at the folder on the table in front of her. She shuffled through a few papers. "Oh, yeah, that's right."

I stifled a groan. What was this woman doing working for a fireworks company if she didn't even know how fireworks worked? I glanced at the doorway, hoping Mrs. Mahoney would walk in.

But then the very thought of Mrs. Mahoney made me begin to feel uneasy. Where was she, anyway? It sure wasn't like her to be late to a meeting, especially not when she was supposed to be in charge.

As that idea ran through my mind I heard a phone ring in the hallway outside. The woman who had answered it opened the door a moment later. "Harold?" she said in a worried tone.

Harold Safer looked at her, and his face went white. "Martha, what is it?"

The woman paused, trembling. "It's—it's the hospital. Agnes Mahoney . . . There was a car crash!"

5

Open Season

By the time I got to River Heights General, there were already several official-looking people huddled in the corridor outside Mrs. Mahoney's hospital room. One of them was Chief McGinnis, head of the River Heights police.

"Got any leads, Nancy?" he asked gruffly.

"Leads? On what?" I asked, confused.

The chief lowered his voice. "This car accident of Mrs. Mahoney's? It was no accident. My men went to the scene of the crash and looked at her car."

I stifled a gasp—both because the stubborn chief had parted with information so easily and because of the magnitude of the crime. "Someone tampered with it?"

He nodded. "The brake pads were loose."

"But who could want to hurt Mrs. Mahoney?" I asked.

Even as I said it, ideas popped into my mind. Art Jeffries had complained about how he'd watched Mrs. Mahoney "run things" around River Heights for years. But Marcus Hammond had looked so satisfied at the meeting last night when the truth about Josiah Mahoney came out. There were definitely a few people who might wish her harm.

The real question was, who felt strongly enough to actually *do* something?

A few minutes later it was my turn to step into Mrs. Mahoney's room. The elderly widow was sitting up in her hospital bed, looking wan but alert. She had combed her gray coiffure to cover most of the bandage around her head. "The doctors say all I've got is a mild concussion," she said in a thin, cheery voice. "With luck, I should still make it to the picnic tomorrow night."

"Now, don't rush things," warned a hovering nurse in white. "We'll keep you under observation for twenty-four hours and then make a decision."

Mrs. Mahoney waved a hand, grand as a queen. I could see she didn't intend to let any mere doctors keep her from presiding over her gala event. She's pretty used to getting her own way by now.

"Mrs. Mahoney, when you started to drive, did

you notice any mechanical problems with your car?" I asked cautiously. I didn't want to scare her.

She frowned. "Problems? No, not at all. In fact, I picked up the car from the service center this morning. It was in perfect running order."

Not so perfect, clearly. "What garage do you use?" I asked.

"Autorama," she said.

Wow, there was a red flag. "You mean the car lot Art Jeffries owns?"

"Yes. He's got a very good mechanic there—a fellow named Mac. Besides, Art gives me a discount."

I bet he does! I thought. "And right afterward you had the accident?"

Mrs. Mahoney turned to face me. "I've told all this to the police already, Nancy. I had several errands to run in town before the meeting. I went to the dry cleaners, the bazaar, and a bakery." She sighed. "I had a dozen beautifully frosted cupcakes on my backseat. Ruined now, I suppose. And I don't even want to think about the condition of that suit I picked up from the cleaners. . . ."

Who cared about the cupcakes? It was that stop at the Jeffries car lot that bothered me!

I knew the police were investigating this crash, but sometimes a private citizen can find out more than a uniformed officer—especially when that private

51

citizen is an innocent-looking teenager who knows what questions to ask. As soon as I left the hospital, I headed right for Jeffries Autorama.

In the central bay of the service center I found a beefy blond guy with MAC embroidered on his gray shirt. "So, Mac," I asked him. "You worked on Mrs. Mahoney's car this morning. What did she bring it in for?"

Mac shrugged. "Oil change, tune-up, a general maintenance check. The works. Why?"

For an instant I wished I'd brought Bess. She's my mechanical expert. Then I remembered why I hadn't—and I felt lousy. Quickly I shuffled it out of my mind. "Did the brake pads need replacing?" I asked.

"Nope." Mac wiped an oil stick on a grease-stained rag from his back pocket. "But I did a routine check on 'em. They were okay."

"And you were the last person to work on it?"

He nodded. "I saw her off in it this morning, around eleven thirty. She likes the personal touch—always brings me a box of cookies. Not that I need it." He grinned, showing big dimples like Ned's.

"I like that old lady," Mac went on. "She drives her car careful. Never speeds, never guns the engine, never races through a light. Never tries to squeeze it into a tiny parking space. That Cadillac of hers is ten years old, but it's in top condition."

That's when I realized I had gotten to him ahead of the police. I felt bad, being the first to tell him about the accident. As I explained I could see tears in his eyes, but I quickly realized they were more for the car than for Mrs. Mahoney. "Any crumpled fenders?" he asked anxiously. "Will it need body work?"

Just then I saw the Autorama tow truck pull in behind Mac with a big navy blue Cadillac on the crane. Mac caught sight of it and turned away. "I can't look," he moaned.

Something told me that Mac could *never* have sabotaged Mrs. Mahoney's car.

Since I seemed to be ahead of the police already, I went on to Rosslyn's Bakery and Martell's Dry Cleaners. Both checked out okay. Clerks there confirmed that Mrs. Mahoney had stopped in, but only quickly—not long enough for anyone to mess up Mac's perfect repairs. The girl at Rosslyn's was so upset at the news of the accident, she even offered to send a dozen richly frosted cupcakes to Mrs. Mahoney at the hospital. I bought a chocolate cupcake myself—part of the investigation, of course.

Still licking chocolate frosting from my fingers, I pulled into my last stop, the sutlers' bazaar in the old

Mahoney warehouse. I guided my car into a space in the gravel parking lot across the street. It was pretty full, I noted—the bazaar must have been doing good business.

I got out, locked my car, and walked over to the attendant—a high school kid squatting on a cinder block with his jacket over his head, trying to escape the light rain that had begun to fall. I paid him a dollar for an hour's parking. "Did you see an old lady in a big navy Cadillac here around twelve thirty today?" I asked.

He squinted at me. "You mean Mrs. Mahoney? Sure, she was here. I always remember Mrs. Mahoney. She's a sweet old lady, and a generous tipper."

I took the hint and slipped another couple of dollars out of my purse. "Did you happen to notice anybody hanging around her car while she was shopping inside?" I asked, handing it over.

He wadded the bills into his jeans pocket. "Funny you should ask. There was a guy prowling around the lot. I was eating lunch—he must have slipped past me. I saw him ducking down around the cars." He gestured toward the northeast corner of the lot. "Near Mrs. Mahoney's Caddy."

I felt my pulse pick up. "What did he look like?"

"Older guy. Gray hair, glasses."

Sounded like Marcus Hammond. "Curly hair?"

"Yeah, as a matter of fact. Skinny guy. Anyway, I went over and asked him what he was doing. He said he was just admiring that classic Cadillac and then he left real quick."

As I headed into the bazaar I brushed the rain off my hair and gave some thought to what the attendant had just told me. I still didn't know much about Marcus Hammond or why he would harm a lady like Mrs. Mahoney, but I figured there were people inside who could tell me.

To my surprise, I ran into Hammond himself, in the first aisle I walked down. He was examining a display of embroidered Confederate insignia. "Hello, Miss Drew," he said. "I was looking for some badges to customize my uniform for the Fourth Mississippi Regiment."

How could I interrogate him without letting on that he was under suspicion? I tried a casual lead-in. "Weren't you here earlier today? Hannah said you and my dad went to rent uniforms."

"Sure. I've been hanging around since ten thirty or eleven," he said. "Lots of clients who used YourHistory.com were coming in and out. It's fun meeting them. I'm sorry now that I didn't go ahead and rent a booth here. I could have done some good business."

"Did you go out for lunch?" I asked.

"I picked up a sandwich," he explained. "And then

I was out in the parking lot a little while."

"You were?" I had to think fast. If he was guilty, why would he freely admit he'd been in the parking lot?

"Sure. I was looking at some merchandise Nathan Emory was selling from the trunk of his car."

"You know Nathan Emory?" Now I really had to think on my feet. Too much information can be as tricky as too little.

"Everyone knows Nathan," Hammond said.

"What was he selling?"

"Old medals, Confederate money—nothing too valuable," he said. He reached in his pocket and pulled out a few oblongs of crumpled paper, printed with ornate designs in blues and mustard colors. "These aren't real, but they're pretty good copies. I thought, if I'm going to pretend I'm a Confederate soldier, let me be one with money in my pocket."

"Good idea," I said. "Did you notice a big dark blue Cadillac out there?"

He nodded. "A real beaut. I admired it on my way back in. Why?"

"Oh, nothing," I said.

"My friend Evaline tells me you're quite an amateur detective." Hammond had changed the subject suddenly. He narrowed his eyes.

Okay, so he knew I was nosing around. I wasn't

going to get anything more from him right now. "Sometimes I do a little detective work . . . if a case pops up," I said with a shrug. "Well, 'bye. Enjoy the bazaar."

"See you at the house," he said as I left. "But not until late. I'm having dinner with Evaline."

I had to check his story, so I circled around to Emory's Armory. Nathan Emory was sitting on a folding chair, eating chow mein from a white cardboard container. "How's business?" I asked.

"Can't complain," he grunted. Clearly he remembered me from yesterday, and he wasn't happy to see me again.

"Marcus Hammond told me you were selling things out of your trunk." Sometimes the best way to get information is to jump right in.

He shook his head. "Don't know him."

"Well, then, how about Martin Halstead?"

Emory's jaw stopped working a second, and then he nodded. "He wanted to see some minnie balls I had. Why? Do you want to buy some?"

I shook my head. "Not today, thanks. But why did you have them in your car?"

He studied the inside of the chow mein carton. "Organizers said I couldn't display them. Someone ratted on me—Todd Willetts, I think." He looked up at me with a hard gaze. "You a friend of Willetts?"

"Not really. I've just met him," I said, sidling away. "Well, thanks for your time."

I wandered off, mind working. So now Marcus Hammond had an alibi for being in the parking lot—if an alibi from a shifty character like Emory was worth anything. But that still didn't prove Hammond hadn't tampered with Mrs. Mahoney's car, did it?

As I stepped back outside the rain was just ending. In the parking lot I saw a plaid sports coat I recalled from yesterday. It belonged to Art Jeffries. Who was he talking to? Curious, I went a few yards down the block to cross the street at a less obvious spot. From that angle I could see a short woman with Jeffries. I'd know that bushy red hair anywhere. Pam Mattei sure did get around.

Just then the setting sun broke through the clouds. I saw a flash, like something metal passing between Jeffries and Mattei. What were they doing?

I had just reached the far sidewalk when I saw Mattei's head duck into a car. I walked faster, but Mattei seemed in quite a hurry herself. The second her car started, she backed it out at a crazy speed. With a clash of gears, she jerked it into drive and sped off. Bits of wet gravel spit at me as I jogged into the lot.

I whipped around and jumped toward Jeffries,

who was getting into his car. I grabbed the side of his door before he could swing it shut. "Mr. Jeffries!" I called out. "I've got some questions for you!"

He scowled. "I'm in a hurry, kid. Got lots to do. With old lady Mahoney out of commission, I have to run everything." He started the engine.

"That's what I wanted to ask you about," I said. "Mrs. Mahoney's car had just been at your service center. I'm wondering what made it crash."

His nostrils flared. "You accusing me of something?" he bellowed. "How dare you? I already talked to the police."

"Please, I'm just gathering information. It couldn't hurt for you to talk to me—"

Jeffries hit the gas. His car lurched forward. I tried to hang on to his half-open car door, but I got yanked off my feet and fell down. Jeffries stomped on the brake to keep from running over me.

My head at ground level, I saw a heavy, grease-coated wrench slide forward from under the driver's seat where Jeffries now sat. I stared at it, amazed at my own dumb luck.

Art Jeffries looked down between his feet and saw it too—and the expression on his face was pure fear.

6

No Stone Unturned

Where'd that wrench come from?" Art Jeffries said.

"From your car," I said, stating the obvious. "I'm going to take a look at it."

Jeffries switched off his car. I got a tissue from my purse and picked up the wrench. I didn't want to blur any fingerprints there might be on it. The thing was already awfully greasy.

If only Bess was here, I wished again. She'd know at once whether this tool could have been used to knock out Mrs. Mahoney's brake pads. I tried to remember what I'd seen her do. I touched the grease coating. It was thin and slippery—not heavy like motor oil. "Brake fluid, all right," I bluffed.

Jeffries believed me. He sighed. "Someone else must have stashed that there," he declared. "Must have been earlier this afternoon. I left the car parked with the window open."

I made a call to Chief McGinnis. That's part of my truce with him: I turn over any useful evidence to the police, and he doesn't give me too hard a time. A cruiser arrived in about three minutes, which gave me a good idea of how important this case was right now.

Driving home, I couldn't forget how mad Art Jeffries had looked as the officers bundled him into their car. Mad and humiliated, but not ashamed. My conscience nagged at me. Art Jeffries was a bully, all right, but was he a saboteur?

Our house was quiet when I got home. I listened carefully, then crept up the carpeted stairs to the guest bedroom. Marcus Hammond had said he wouldn't be back until later. That gave me enough time to sniff around. Maybe Hammond hadn't tampered with the car, but I still had a lot of nagging questions about him, and it was time to get them answered.

I knew that guest room well, but it seemed almost alien now. A zippered black canvas suitcase sat on the cedar chest. A tan windbreaker hung over the back of a chair. A pair of ankle boots were set neatly, side by side, below it. On the bedside table sat a paperback thriller that could have been bought at any airport newsstand.

Usually I don't mind inspecting somebody's stuff

as part of an investigation, but it felt weird this time. After all, Mr. Hammond was a guest in our house. As his host, I was supposed to respect his privacy—and there I was, unzipping the suitcase to paw through his clothes.

The one thing that struck me was how bland Hammond's clothes were—plain cotton, conservative styles, and labels I didn't recognize. They all looked new, as if he'd just bought them; a few even had price tags. I dug into the side pockets, hoping for personal documents, but I found nothing. I checked the outside handle of the suitcase to see which name was printed on the ID tag—Marcus Hammond or Martin Halstead. But the tag had been left blank, and there were no airport tags to tell me where our guest had traveled lately.

I went into the bathroom to check the prescription labels on his toiletries, but he had no prescription medicines at all, just toothpaste, a toothbrush, dental floss, a hairbrush, a disposable razor, some shaving cream, and deodorant. How boring!

Just then I heard the downstairs door slam and Hannah's voice call out, "Nancy? I'm back." I grabbed Hammond's hairbrush and dashed out into the hall. Hannah would be furious if she caught me snooping on our guest. "Up here!" I called from the landing. "Just about to take a shower!"

Once in my room, I turned on the shower to distract Hannah, then got out my fingerprint kit. I took a sample of Mr. Hammond's fingerprints from the brush, along with a few hairs for chemical analysis. But as I tiptoed barefoot into his room to replace the brush, I felt discouraged. Prints and hairs wouldn't help me much. Verifying his DNA was easy. But what I needed was to figure out if he had a motive to hurt Mrs. Mahoney.

Dad was working late that night, so Hannah and I ate dinner in the kitchen. "It seems awfully quiet tonight," Hannah said.

"Yeah, I know," I agreed with a sigh. I took a bite of Hannah's broccoli-cheese casserole, one of my favorites. It didn't taste as delicious as usual, but then, I wasn't as hungry as usual. "Normally when Dad works late, we have Bess or George over—or both," I pointed out. I swallowed hard, trying to get rid of the lump of loneliness in my throat.

"No brooding at the dinner table," Hannah said firmly. "Let's talk about something else. Did you hear that poor Mrs. Mahoney crashed into a concrete barrier and went to the hospital?"

I roused myself. "Yes, I saw her," I said. "There was something funny about her brakes. Art Jeffries was taken in for questioning."

Hannah's eyes opened wide. "My goodness! And

you act like it's no big deal. Why, Art Jeffries is a real big shot these days, what with all the reenactment plans. And he's been arrested?"

The wall phone started ringing. "Not arrested, just questioned," I said. "Big difference." I picked up the phone, hoping it was Bess or George calling to say they were sorry.

"Nancy? It's Charlie Adams."

"Charlie?" I said. "This is a switch, you calling me. Don't tell me *you* need a tow!"

Charlie chuckled, but he sounded preoccupied. "Nope, but Nancy, I could use your help."

"It's about time you let me pay you back for all the help you've given me," I said. "What's up?"

"Well, you see—" He paused, lowering his voice. "I'm out at the reenactment site. I was here all day, fixing up the landscape, like I told you. I came back after work—I went home, but I forgot my toolbox, so I came back. As I drove up I saw some flashlights in the woods."

"Any other cars in the parking lot?" I asked.

"Not a one," he said. "At first I figured it was just kids messing around, so I called out. But no one answered, and the flashlights switched off. If they were kids, they would have answered, wouldn't they? I'm just thinking . . . well, I wouldn't want anyone to sabotage the site. We've worked so hard to keep it safe and authentic."

That word, *sabotage*, got my attention. If somebody could sabotage an old lady's car, someone could certainly sabotage the reenactment site. And considering how many people in town were looking forward to this event on Saturday—

"Stay right there, Charlie. I'm coming," I said.

As I pulled into the Riverside Park parking lot I cut my engine and let my car coast to a stop. No point in letting our intruders know another car had arrived. Though it was dark, there was enough light from stars and distant streetlights for me to spot the dark shape of Charlie Adams and his truck across the lot.

"The lights came from over there," Charlie whispered, gesturing in the dark as I joined him.

"Have they shown up again since you called me?"

Charlie shook his head. "No lights, no sounds, nothing. And you know how this park is laid out. There's river on three sides, and the wall along the road is too high to climb. Anyone who leaves has to come out this entrance."

"Unless they want to jump off the bluffs into the Muskoka," I pointed out.

Charlie snorted. "If they'd tried that, I would have

heard screams. Those bluffs are treacherous."

I pulled a low-beam flashlight out of my pocket. "Well, no reason for us to whisper and creep around," I said in a normal voice. "We have a right to be here. They don't. And if someone went into those woods, they must have left some trace."

Luckily for us, the rain that afternoon had left the ground soft, and the bulldozers had exposed fresh layers of soil everywhere. Not far from the parking lot, some clear footprints veered off the paved path. "Was everyone on the crew today wearing work boots?" I asked Charlie.

He thought before he answered. "Yes, even the designers. There's so much heavy equipment around, it wouldn't be safe to wear street shoes."

"Well, somebody wore street shoes," I said, shining my light on the prints. One set had made smooth indentations, not the waffle treads of work boots. And the other prints consisted of a triangle and a small circle. "A woman's high heels," I said.

"Not very practical for the woods," Charlie commented.

Who could have been walking there? Pam Mattei was a good bet—a woman that short would most likely wear high heels a lot. But if she'd come that evening after the crew left, she couldn't have been with Art Jeffries—he was probably still at the police station, being questioned. Who else? Nathan Emory? Marcus Hammond? He had told me not to expect him until later. I wished now that I had taken an impression of his boots when I had the chance—then I'd have an idea if the size matched these prints. I measured the muddy impressions anyway. They looked like they'd match a size ten or ten and a half shoe.

Then an image flashed through my mind: Art Jeffries and Pam Mattei, passing something metal between them in the parking lot this afternoon. Was it a shovel? "Let's see if anybody has been digging," I said, following the prints across the leveled field.

Close to the edge of the woods I shone my light on a few mounds of freshly turned earth. I knelt, studying them.

"I don't recall this area being marked on the plans," Charlie said.

"What *is* supposed to be around here?"

"The weapons depot for the Confederate army," Charlie said. "We're building a shed tomorrow, about ten yards from here. It's important to the battle—at Black Creek, the Union blew up the Confederate ammunition supply."

"Blew up?" I shivered.

"But we weren't digging here today," Charlie said. "And this wasn't done with the big earthmovers we were using. This hole was made with a small shovel."

We both had the same idea. We started feeling around in the grass and bushes nearby. It wasn't long before Charlie called out, "Nailed it!" He rose from a patch of bushes, holding up a garden shovel with a sharp point.

I shone the light on it. There was a film of gray dust on the point, unlike the crumbly reddish soil we were standing on. I swiped some off with my finger and sniffed it.

I knew that sulphur smell. Gunpowder!

"Looks like someone may have planted explosives underfoot," I said, feeling uneasy. "If those were set off during the reenactment—"

"I'll see that it's dug up tomorrow, soon as there's light," Charlie said. "And maybe the police can get fingerprints off this shovel."

"Good idea," I said. "Let's go back to the parking area to look for tire tracks. That may give us another clue."

As we trooped back, the nighttime cold and damp were beginning to sink into my bones. I didn't feel like waiting any longer for our phantom intruders. Anyway, by then they might have crept out the entrance without our seeing them.

Just then I heard a tinkling crash ahead in the lot. My heart jumped as I ran toward it, Charlie right behind me.

The rising moon glittered on my windshield—and its intricate spiderweb of shattered glass. Shoot! I could hear an engine rev up on the road outside the park, followed by the screech of wheels.

A big gray rock, about eight inches across, sat on the moon-kissed pavement beside my car. I knelt to pick it up.

A piece of paper was wrapped around the rock, held on with a greasy rubber band. I peeled it off and unfolded it.

In a demented scrawl, someone had written a hateful message: REBEL SCUM MUST DIE.

7

Rockets' Red Glare

Over Charlie's protests, I drove myself home. Sure, it was hard avoiding oncoming cars when their headlights shone into my smashed windshield, reflecting light everywhere. But I just couldn't listen to Charlie fuss over me and worry whether I could drive okay. Like I told him, the rock through my windshield didn't bother me—I just wished it had yielded a clue that led somewhere.

Mr. Hammond's car—a bronze compact that looked about four or five years old—was sitting at the curb in front of our house when I pulled into the driveway. I hurried to the front door, eager to ask him a few questions.

Inside, I checked whether he had left muddy shoe

prints on the hall carpet, but there was nothing. I looked upstairs, and I could see that the guest room door was already firmly closed. I could only assume that our guest had already come home and gone to bed. I'd have to wait until morning to question Hammond.

Why was I so eager to pin something on Marcus Hammond? I realized I had no idea. I couldn't even say *what* I was trying to pin on him! Mrs. Mahoney's car crash? Burying explosives at the battle site?

I changed into pajamas automatically, mulling over this case—if it really was a case. From what I could tell, Hammond had the means, and probably the opportunity, for both those acts. But then, so did Pam Mattei, Nathan Emory, and Art Jeffries—a whole lineup of people I didn't trust. And what motive did any of them have? Finding a motive was key.

Hammond was an old friend of Evaline Waters. Shouldn't that make me trust him?

The way I figured it, Hammond was like a shadowy figure you sometimes spot in the background of a crime scene photo. For some reason, my eye was drawn straight to him. And every time I looked at the picture, that was all I could see.

Up until then I hadn't even thought I was particularly tired. But ten seconds after I crawled into bed and my head hit the pillow, I was out like a light.

. . . .

I was up by seven fifteen next morning, but it still wasn't early enough to catch Hammond. The guest room was open and empty when I stepped out of my room, and a glance out the window showed me that his little bronze car was already gone.

I couldn't resist—I had to go search his room again. I went straight for his other pair of shoes, under the chair. They were smooth-soled loafers, size ten and a half, but they didn't have a trace of mud on them. Maybe he'd cleaned them off? I was looking for the wastebasket to check for muddy tissues when Hannah walked in.

"Lost something, Nancy?" she asked pointedly. "I don't think Mr. Hammond would appreciate you being in here."

I saw the empty wastebasket in her hand. I didn't dare ask if she'd found anything muddy in it. "Uh, I was . . ." I made up a story on the spot. "I was about to do some laundry, and I thought I'd check if Mr. Hammond had anything to throw in."

"Too late. I just threw his clothes into the washer," she said, hands on her hips.

"I guess they got dirty yesterday in the rain," I suggested, fishing for information.

Hannah shook her head. "Not that I noticed. He seems a tidy man—a real gentleman. It's a pleasure having him here." She gave me a sharp look. "Everything okay with Charlie? You came home late."

"He's fine," I said. "What's for breakfast?"

Downstairs, while Hannah was serving up a bowl of blueberry granola, I used the hall phone to call Chief McGinnis. I told him about the flashlights in the woods. "You saw these lights yourself?" he asked in a testy voice.

"No, Charlie did," I answered. "But I trust his story absolutely. And I did see footprints, and some unauthorized digging."

"I'll bet when Charlie gets to work today, he'll find out it was all part of the project," the chief growled. "And no harm done."

"No harm?" I echoed. "Chief, someone threw a rock at my car last night, with a note that said, 'Rebel scum must die.' If I'd been in the car—"

He cut me off. "But you weren't. Whoever threw that rock knew that. It was just a prank—maybe one of your friends, teasing you for signing up to fight with the Confederates."

I instantly thought of Bess and George, but I couldn't see either of them playing such a dangerous trick on anyone, let alone on me.

"Now, Nancy," the chief went on, "do me a favor and stop prying. There's no case here. Like Mrs. Mahoney's accident yesterday—it looks like it was

73

just an accident. My men asked around and they didn't find any shady evidence."

"What about Art Jeffries and the wrench in his car?"

"The man runs an auto dealership. Of course he has tools in his car!" McGinnis exploded. "But thanks to you, I had to embarrass him by taking him in for questioning. That was not pleasant, believe me. Art Jeffries is our Union general for the reenactment tomorrow. He's my commanding officer. He deserves respect. So please, stay off his back."

Hanging up, I mulled over the situation. I guessed Art Jeffries had raked the chief over the coals last night. That was too bad for the chief, but it still didn't mean there was no case, did it?

Usually I try to cooperate with Chief McGinnis. Clearly, I couldn't this time.

First thing I had to do was get my windshield fixed. I knew Charlie was busy at the battlefield instead of his garage, so I drove to Jeffries Autorama. A big place like that was likely to have parts, even for an unusual car like mine. Besides, I liked Mac, the mechanic. And . . . well, it wouldn't hurt for me to see what Art Jeffries was up to.

Mac remembered me from the day before and was eager to help get my car fixed. "It'll be done by four o'clock," he promised, slapping a repair order on the broken windshield. "Can I give you a loaner for the day?" he asked, pointing to a row of used cars.

I looked over to where he pointed. They were all gas guzzlers, of course, but still, I needed transportation. I accepted a set of keys from Mac.

As I was getting into the loaner car, I saw Pam Mattei's red hair vanishing into the showroom. I jumped right back out of the car and headed after her.

I stopped her just as she reached Art Jeffries's glass office door. "Ms. Mattei?" I called out. As she turned I saw Jeffries inside his office, rising from his desk. I hurried to her side to draw her away. "Ms. Mattei, I was wondering if you've been out to Riverside Park, to the battle site," I began. "Last night I saw footprints there—high heels—"

She flashed me her usual hard, bright smile. "Sure, I was there," she admitted. "We're going back this morning, too. By the time we got there last night, it was too dark to see. Our meeting got pushed back. Art had unexpected business downtown."

She nodded to Jeffries, who glowered at us from his office doorway. "Unexpected business?" So Jeffries hadn't admitted to her that he was at the police station! That sure didn't make it look like they were in cahoots. But then, why was he hiding the fact that he'd been questioned by the cops?

"I thought you were only involved with the fire-works at the picnic," I said to Ms. Mattei.

"That was under the original contract," Jeffries butted in to our conversation. "But after Pam arrived, I got an idea for some special effects to add to the battle. We're going to simulate the explosion of the rebs' ammo dump."

Mattei gave me another teeth-baring smile. "Nothing too elaborate—just some red and orange dazzles. We are the explosives experts, after all."

I thought fast, trying to dredge up my high school chemistry. "And you brought extra supplies of, uh, copper and barium powders to do that sort of effect?" I asked. Mattei nodded energetically. "Well, it sounds like it'll look really cool," I said, backing away. "Good luck."

Fifteen minutes later I was home and digging out my old chemistry textbook. I quickly found the table I was looking for. Just as I remembered: Copper and barium give off blue and green colors when they're ignited. To get red you'd need lithium. Some form of carbon, like charcoal, would produce orange.

I slammed the book shut. Whoever said those chemistry lessons would never come in handy?

Now I had a lead to track down. Pam Mattei should have known which powders they'd be using, if she was the explosives expert she claimed to be.

I picked up the phone and made a few calls until I reached Dawn's Early Light Productions in Long Island City, New York. A young woman in the personnel department confirmed that Pam Mattei was an employee. "I had a friend of that name in college," I fibbed. "I hope it's the same person. How long has she been there?"

"Only a few months," she said. "She just moved here."

"From where?" I asked.

"Some place upstate," the woman said vaguely. Her voice faded as she asked someone at her end, "You know Pam? Where'd she used to live?" There was a muffled answer, then she said into the phone, "Potsdam."

I gulped. Potsdam, New York . . . the same town as Marcus Hammond. Or should I say Martin Halstead?

"Nancy, you and Deirdre take the west gate," Harold Safer told us. "When George and Bess arrive, I'll set them up at the east gate."

I didn't dare argue, or I'd make Deirdre mad. But trooping after her to the west gate, I felt distinctly annoyed. I'd been counting on chatting with Bess and George at the picnic while we handed out the glow-in-the-dark necklaces. It would have been a perfect opportunity for us to resolve our differences.

Now here I was stuck at the other end of the park—and with Deirdre, too!

I consoled myself with the thought that standing at the gate gave me a good vantage point for watching the various suspects in the case—this case-that-wasn't-a-case, as the chief kept telling me. It was looking less like a case all the time, I had to admit. Charlie had called me that afternoon to report that the digging in Riverside Park was a late change to the battle plan—no sabotage after all. I guess that let Pam Mattei off the hook. But I could still be suspicious about Mrs. Mahoney's accident, couldn't I?

I felt a pain in my stomach when I saw Evaline Waters walk in, arm in arm with Marcus Hammond. She wore a crisp white blouse, a long flowered skirt, and a dreamy look on her face. I realized that I'd never seen her look so happy, and I could tell it was because of Marcus Hammond. He acted really attentive, holding her arm tight and leaning close to her. But for a guy with nothing on his conscience, he seemed to be peering around a lot .

Their entrance was overshadowed by the grand entrance Mrs. Mahoney made, escorted into the park by the mayor. A buzz of chatter rose around her as she halted by the picnic shelter. Everyone seemed to have heard about her car accident and knew she had been in the hospital. From the gleam in her eye, I guessed she'd used a lot of persuasion on her doctors to get released so soon.

I saw Nathan Emory break through the crowd around her. "Mrs. Mahoney," he said, "best wishes from the merchants at the sutlers' bazaar. We're so grateful for all you've done. On their behalf, I offer this token of our appreciation." He held out a lumpy parcel covered in silvery paper.

With a royal smile Mrs. Mahoney took it and fumbled with the wrapping. "What is it?" she asked.

Emory helped her with the last bits of wrapping. "An authentic Confederate water canteen," he explained. "See the engraving? It was from the Seventeenth Georgia Regiment. This is a rare piece."

"And so beautiful," Mrs. Mahoney said. "I hardly deserve it."

"Why, Agnes," the mayor said, "if it hadn't been for you, this reenactment would never have happened. It was your idea in the first place."

"Nonsense," Mrs. Mahoney said. "It was Evaline Waters who first brought the society this idea. She knew we were looking for a way to commemorate our anniversary. Evaline, where are you, dear? This memento really should be yours."

Ms. Waters stepped modestly forward. "It was just a notion I had," she said, taking the canteen. "You and the society put the plan into action."

"But no one knew before that River Heights men had fought at Black Creek," the mayor pointed out. "What inspired you to research that battle?"

Evaline turned around to look for Marcus Hammond. Maybe it was my imagination, but I thought I saw him scowl and grab her elbow. What was that about? Didn't he want her to get the attention she deserved?

"Oh, n-nothing," she stammered, turning back to the mayor. "Just an old librarian poking around in books. Th-thanks again." She turned quickly and disappeared with Hammond into the crowd.

"Wow, that was weird," I murmured to myself.

Deirdre, beside me, shrugged. "Mousy old maids like her hate the spotlight," she scoffed. "Well, I'm outta here." She tossed her last few necklaces on a nearby picnic table and strolled off.

She had a point—just about everyone who wanted a necklace had one. It was definitely time to go find George and Bess. As I headed for the east gate, Ned fell into step beside me. "There goes Nancy Drew with her confident stride," he teased me.

"I don't feel so confident," I admitted. "I'm on my way to talk things out with the girls."

Ned threw a sympathetic arm around my shoulder. "Relax. It's only George and Bess. They're probably just waiting for you to make the first move. They'll be so glad to see you—"

"Nancy, Nancy! At *last* I found you," Harold Safer cried out, stepping in front of us. "We've got a problem."

I turned to him, half annoyed and half relieved to put off facing my friends. "What is it?"

"Follow me." Harold threaded his way through the crowd. I had to work to keep up.

We went past some wooden barriers and down a slope to the riverbank. He pointed to two barges bobbing in the water, their decks covered with troughs of sand. Rows of metal canisters were propped at an angle in the sand. "Do you see anyone there?"

I blinked. "No—no one."

"Exactly!" He crossed his arms. "Where is the fireworks crew? There were three of them on that barge earlier. Here I leave for just a *minute* to watch the sunset, and *poof!* they vanish."

I scanned the scene. "That rowboat," I said, pointing to a small boat rocking in the water. "Is that theirs?"

He nodded. "I guess so! But why would they row ashore now? The fireworks are set to go off in fifteen minutes!"

I turned to Ned. "Got it covered, Nan," he said,

reading my mind. He strode up the bank to check around onshore for the crew.

Meanwhile Harold and I swiftly rowed out to the barges. Stepping onto the deck, I could see how good the sand was at holding the metal rockets in place. Multicolored strands of wire snaked from one device to another. The deepening dusk made it hard to see, but here and there gleamed a few bare points of freshly cut copper wires. Someone had clipped them!

I knelt to examine one mortar. The sand packed around it had been disturbed recently. Studying the steel launching tube, I noticed that it pointed toward shore, not up to the sky like the others.

"I don't know beans about fireworks," Harold said in a low voice, "but even a technophobe like me could see that someone's tampered with this setup."

A prickle of fear crept up my neck. "Maybe we should abort the display."

Harold winced. "I would, but it's computer programmed." He gestured toward a black box at one end of the barge. "I have no idea how to stop it."

George. We had to find George! But even if I was on speaking terms with her, could I get her to the barge on time?

My answer came a second later, as a tiny yellow light on the computer switched to green. At the far end of the barge, a spark suddenly fizzed at the base of the farthest mortar.

Inside the steel launching tube, a powder charge ignited. And with a screaming whistle, the first rocket soared into the night sky.

8

Double Trouble

Quick, Harold, how much time have we got before this section of the explosives is set to fire?" I demanded.

He rubbed his brow anxiously. "I have no idea. Pam gave me a run-through of the whole show, but I didn't listen too hard. I figured it was in the experts' hands."

A chrysanthemum-shaped purple light exploded in the sky. A chorus of approving *aahhs* rose from the crowd onshore.

"We've got to clear out the picnic grounds, *now*," I decided. I grabbed Harold by the shoulders and shoved him toward the rowboat, scolding myself for leaving my cell phone in my car.

Luckily we weren't far offshore. A few hard oar strokes was all we needed to reach the bank. As the second firework burst in the sky, Harold shouted frantically into his walkie-talkie. "Fire crew, fire crew, come in, please! This is Safer."

As we landed, the firefighters on duty answered with a buzz of static. Climbing up the riverbank, I could hear him arguing. "Believe me, it's an emergency. No time to explain—just clear the picnic area!"

At the top of the bank I saw a bunch of firefighters huddled uncertainly next to their truck. Then three men in loose black clothing hurtled past them. "Who executed the start command already?" one of them shouted.

"Why didn't that blue whizzer go off yet?" a second one yelled. "I don't like the looks of this malfunction!"

That had to be the pyrotechnical crew. The fire captain, seeing them so frantic, seemed to suddenly take the situation seriously. He hoisted his bullhorn. "Attention, attention," he announced to the picnickers. "The grove must be evacuated immediately!"

The puzzled crowd didn't react at first. Everyone was still too busy gaping at the sky, filled now with a yellow palm-tree effect. But the firefighters, once in action, were effective. I was impressed by how calm they were, ushering people toward the exits. In the distance I heard the siren of an additional truck arriving to help as an orange-and-blue roundel popped in the sky.

Following the crowd, I looked for Ned, George, Bess, anyone I knew. As we passed a row of picnic tables, I saw Ms. Waters's prize canteen lying alone on a table. I tried to step aside to grab it, but I was pushed hard from behind. The human tide swept me toward the park gates.

And then, behind me, I heard a horrible dragon-like hiss. I twisted around to see a metal rocket whizzing across the park's central pond, angling into the picnic area. The same area that, a minute and a half ago, had been filled with people!

Trailing a hot stream of purple sparks, the blazing shell struck the roof of a picnic shelter and burst into flame.

That was when the crowd lost it. Folks panicked, stampeding every which way. I felt a hard elbow in my ribs. Someone else stomped on my ankle. I scooped up a little girl in front of me just in time to keep her from being trampled.

Then, as if by magic, the park floodlights snapped on. The fire captain yelled into his bullhorn, "Calm down, folks. You've got lots of time. The fireworks show has been terminated." I peered out at the barge.

The three men in black were clapping each other on the shoulders, relieved.

Great. But why weren't they there earlier, when they could have prevented this mess?

Fortunately the crowd did seem to relax. I spotted the little girl's parents and returned her to them. Then I stood in the shelter of a huge old elm tree, looking for a few suspects. If this hadn't been a case before, it sure was now.

I'd seen Marcus Hammond earlier, but was he still on the scene? What about Art Jeffries? Nathan Emory? And Pam Mattei? Considering that she was the executive in charge of the fireworks, her absence was extremely suspicious.

Chief McGinnis pulled up in a black-and-white squad car. As I headed toward him I was surprised to see Art Jeffries climb out of the squad car too. "We were at our final battlefield planning meeting," the chief said to me, "when I got the radio call. Mr. Jeffries left with me. Where's Harold Safer?"

"Over by the blaze, talking to the fire captain," I said, waving in their direction. "But what I'm wondering is, where is Ms. Mattei?"

Art Jeffries gave me a weary look. "She was at our meeting. We were working out our mock ammo explosion, trying to make sure it would be handled . . .

safely." His mouth tightened as he saw the damage to the picnic shelter. "She figured her crew would handle this event. Guess she was wrong. Where are they?"

"They weren't on the barge when the display ignited," I said. "I know it was all computer programmed, but I assumed they'd be there—"

"And usually we would be," spoke up one of the men in black. I turned to see the three of them behind me. "But the timer was evidently reset for ten minutes sooner. I don't know who did that."

"Wilson got a call that his car's security alarm had gone off," piped up the man next to him. "He carries lots of explosives in his trunk—we were worried that someone was breaking in. So we all three went to investigate."

"We thought we'd have time. It was still twenty minutes before the planned ignition time," explained Wilson.

"Who called you about the alarm?" I asked.

The crew glanced at one another blankly. "He said he was the police officer at the parking lot," Wilson recalled.

"How did he have your cell phone number?" I asked.

Wilson shrugged, looking embarrassed. "Now that I think about it, that was kind of fishy. But at the time, I was only thinking about those explosives."

So it had been a man's voice on that anonymous phone call. That let Pam Mattei off the hook, though as their boss, she wouldn't have needed an elaborate ruse if she'd wanted to get the crew off the barge.

The chief took Wilson's cell phone and located the number shown for that last received call so his staff could run a trace. Meanwhile I ran to my car to get my own cell phone. By now the parking lot was emptying out. Curious as they were, the picnic-goers had followed orders and headed home to safety. The only people left in the park were firefighters, the fireworks technicians, the police, and an ambulance crew that had arrived in case of injuries.

My first call was home to Hannah. I was relieved to learn that she and Dad had decided to skip the picnic after all. But I didn't like the fact that Mr. Hammond hadn't come home yet.

Next I called Evaline Waters's house. No answer. It had been half an hour since the picnickers were sent away—plenty of time for Marcus and Evaline to return home. Of course, they could have gone out for a late dinner at a restaurant. But I thought I'd feel a lot better if I knew where they were. I left a message on Evaline's machine to call me.

When I got off the phone, I went to find Chief McGinnis. His men had been working the phones too, trying to locate several people they regarded as suspects. "Nancy, do you know anything about this Nathan Emory guy?" the chief asked me, consulting a pad of notes he had been taking.

I frowned. "He tried to stiff my dad on a rifle," I said. "And I heard that the bazaar organizers reprimanded him for displaying a certain type of merchandise—something called a minnie ball. Yeah, I saw him here earlier."

"That's what the mayor said—he presented some gift to Mrs. Mahoney," the chief said, jotting down my information. "Well, we tried to contact him for questioning, and he seems to have vanished."

That didn't sound good. "What do you mean?"

"He checked out of his hotel at eight this evening, even though he had booked it through Sunday morning."

"But why leave town tonight—on the eve of the battle?" I asked, puzzled.

The chief shrugged. "I'd better put out a bulletin for the state police to watch for his car."

"Chief!" a member of the fire crew shouted. "You'd better come over and see this!"

I made sure I was right behind him.

The area where the picnic shelter had been was a disaster. We found a jagged hole in the roof, charred stumps of picnic tables, half-melted steel pipes, and a cracked and blackened slab of concrete. Leaves had been singed off nearby trees, but the firefighters' quick actions had saved the trees themselves.

The fire captain pointed to a burned patch of cement at the side of the shelter. Peering over McGinnis's shoulder, I saw what they were looking at.

On the ruined cement lay a round gray metal object, eight inches across, dented and half-covered with black greasy powder. A puddle of what looked like water had dribbled from it onto the pavement.

It was the antique Confederate canteen that Nathan Emory had given Mrs. Mahoney, who had then given it to Evaline Waters!

And beside the puddle, on the strafed soil, a skinny gray-striped cat lay writhing in pain. Its swollen stomach heaved in and out, as if convulsed with pain. I got closer and saw that, beneath its mangy fur, the cat's skin was flushed a deep pink. It needed immediate help.

"Just some stray cat—who knows what's made it sick," I heard a firefighter say.

Whispering to try to calm the poor cat, I reached over and picked up the canteen. Its metal was still hot from the explosion, but I held it long enough to sniff the open mouth.

That faint almond scent—I'd know it anywhere.

Cyanide.

9

With Every Intent

To be sure, I dabbed my finger into the puddle of water beside the canteen and sniffed. It was cyanide, all right.

"Looks like the cat lapped up some poison," I said, feeling sick at heart. "Poor thing."

"Poison—in that canteen?" Chief McGinnis asked. As a firefighter scooped up the cat to make its last moments more comfortable, the chief and I traded glances. I knew he was thinking what I was thinking. Had anyone else drunk from that canteen?

"The cat couldn't have screwed off the top to this canteen—some person did," I pointed out. "And it wouldn't take a very big drink to get a fatal amount of cyanide. It's a nasty poison, and it works fast.

Whoever drank this would need medical attention immediately—within half an hour of ingesting it."

"That stampede earlier," the fire captain said. "Someone in distress might have been pushed into the woods and collapsed. He—"

"Or *she*—," I broke in. I thought of the phone ringing, unanswered, at Ms. Waters's house.

That was all the firefighters needed. A dozen of them, gripping axes and walkie-talkies, fanned out and plunged into the woods.

"Let's get an antidote ready," I said, turning to one of the EMTs who'd arrived in the ambulance. Lucky they were still there. "A dose of amyl nitrate, then a stomach pump, then artificial respiration."

The young man nodded. "We'll have an oxygen mask hooked up and ready. Anything else?"

"Injections of sodium nitrite and sodium thiosulfate, I think," I said, remembering what I'd seen on a case not too long ago. "But you'd better look it up in your manual—get the right concentrations."

The med techs were on it at once. I turned back to Chief McGinnis. "People can survive cyanide poisoning," I said, trying to reassure both of us. "If they last four hours after swallowing it, they usually recover, depending on how much they swallowed, and if they're in good health—"

"You're thinking of Agnes Mahoney," Chief McGinnis guessed. "Wasn't this the memento that Emory guy gave her?"

I replayed the scene in my mind. "Yes. But Nathan Emory made a show of presenting the canteen to her. If he knew cyanide was inside, he wouldn't let everyone see him with it. Why run that risk?"

The chief shook his head. "Beats me. But the woman had a suspicious car accident yesterday. Looks to me like someone's out to get her."

"But Mrs. Mahoney didn't keep the canteen," I told him. "She gave it to Evaline Waters." I twisted my hands, looking anxiously toward the woods.

He looked startled. "The librarian?"

I nodded. "Evidently she was the first one to suggest to the historical society that they sponsor a reenactment of the Battle of Black Creek."

Chief McGinnis pushed his hat back on his head. "So the poison could have been given to the wrong victim?"

Suddenly I got a mental flash of Marcus Hammond, hustling Ms. Waters away after she'd been given the canteen. At the time, I'd assumed he just didn't want her getting attention for the reenactment idea. But did he have another motive? *Had he known that there was poison in the canteen?*

Before I could tell the chief about Hammond, a

police officer behind me interrupted. "Look who we found, Chief," he said.

I whirled around, hoping to see Evaline Waters being carried to safety. Instead I saw Nathan Emory escorted by two police officers, his khakis looking rumpled and his hands handcuffed in front. "This is Emory, the weapons salesman," the officer said.

Chief McGinnis's eyes narrowed. "You moved out of your hotel in an awful hurry, pal. Care to tell us why you were leaving town?"

Emory rolled his eyes. "Like I was telling these good officers, I wasn't leaving town," he explained. "Why would I leave town before battle day? That's my big moneymaker. It's just that a friend of mine—a fellow sutler—suggested I move into his hotel room to save money. Business was a little off, so it seemed a good idea."

"Check out his story," McGinnis ordered one of the apprehending officers. "Can you identify this?" the chief asked Emory, holding up the canteen.

Emory looked at it, wincing to see the dents and the coating of burned powder. "Sure. It's a standard issue water canteen from the Seventeenth Georgia Regiment, circa 1863. A genuine antique, from my collection. I gave it to Mrs. Mahoney tonight as a memento. But what happened to it?"

"Damaged in the fireworks blast," the chief said.

"When you gave it to Mrs. Mahoney, was it empty?"

Emory looked baffled. "Of course. It's a valuable antique, not a common drinking vessel. I wouldn't trust that old metal alloy—it might have lead in it. These were made long before we knew the health risks of lead."

"Could someone else have filled it without you knowing it?" I asked.

Emory glanced nervously at me. He was probably surprised to see this teenager helping the police in their inquiry—I get that a lot. "I'd have noticed if it was full," he said with an edge of sarcasm. "It would have felt heavy. I would have heard water sloshing inside. Hey, what's this about? I thought you were investigating a fireworks accident."

"We thought so too," the chief said curtly. "Mr. Emory, we'll need a sworn statement. Officer Price will take you downtown."

Emory was led away, protesting. Chief McGinnis took off his hat and wiped his forehead. "So, suppose someone else put in the cyanide later . . ."

"After Evaline Waters got the canteen." I finished his thought. "So it looks like it wasn't intended for Mrs. Mahoney. I remember now, I saw the canteen lying on a picnic table during the evacuation from the park. I don't know if it was full or empty

96

then, but anyone could have put poison in it."

He sighed, setting his hat back on his head. "Which means this is a separate crime from Mrs. Mahoney's accident. Two crimes to solve."

I counted them on my fingers. "Mrs. Mahoney's accident is one. The poisoning is two. The fireworks sabotage . . . three. And don't forget the person who threw a rock through my windshield last night."

Chief McGinnis tilted his head skeptically. "Now, that might just have been some punk kids."

"I don't think so," I insisted. "Look—four crimes, four different targets. But it's all circling around the reenactment. What if the real target is the reenactment itself?"

The chief frowned, pulling on his lower lip. "You may have something there. The note on the rock mentioned 'rebel scum,' and this canteen is from a Confederate regiment. Maybe someone on the Southern team is trying to threaten the Northern forces."

That remark really threw me. "Why would you think that?" I blurted out. "The message to me said, 'Rebel scum must die.' That's what a Union soldier would say. And suppose someone from the North left that canteen here to frame the Confederates."

McGinnis's eyes flashed. "What are you implying? It's like Art Jeffries said to me last night: The Union forces tend to be the decent citizens around town, but folks who join the Confederates are born trouble-makers."

"Like me and my dad?" I shot back, outraged.

Before my anger took over, I shook myself. "Wow, this is crazy," I said. "Everybody in town is taking this battle way too seriously."

Chief McGinnis sighed. "Sorry, Nancy. You're right. Got to keep a clear head."

"Let's assume it's the reenactment itself they're try-ing to ruin," I suggested, trying to get back on track. "Casting suspicions on both sides is the best way to do that, isn't it?"

Chief McGinnis nodded. "It is. We'll make that our working hypothesis," he agreed. "Now I'll go check up on some of these leads—the number on Wilson's cell phone, fingerprints on the fireworks command keyboard."

Saying good night, I headed back to my car, still shaken by my near-argument with the chief. If I could get so emotional with McGinnis over this battle stuff, no wonder tempers had gotten out of hand with Bess and George.

I was halfway home before I remembered that I hadn't mentioned Marcus Hammond to the chief. I could have kicked myself. And I even had a set of his fingerprints—surely that would be of use to the police! I'd have to call the chief first thing in the morning.

The phone was ringing as I came in the front door. "I'll get it," I yelled, hoping it was George or Bess. Who else would call this late at night?

But when I answered the phone, the voice at the other end was Evaline Waters. "Ms. Waters, you're okay!" I said, flooded with relief.

"Well, yes, I am," she said in a tight voice. "I'm returning your call from earlier this evening."

I paused, confused. Then I remembered calling her after the fireworks crash, to check on Marcus Hammond's whereabouts. I'd gotten so worried over the cyanide poisoning, I'd completely forgotten the fireworks sabotage. My instincts told me not to mention the cyanide to Ms. Waters, though, now that I knew she was safe.

"I just wanted to make sure Mr. Hammond got you home okay," I said. "That was a lot of confusion at the park."

She paused. "Mr. Hammond and I left before the fireworks," she said. Weird—she almost sounded like a robot. "We had a quiet dinner alone. He has been with me all evening. Well, good night." And she hung up.

As I put the receiver back in the cradle, my dad appeared in the archway to our living room. "Nancy? Who was that?" he asked.

"Evaline Waters," I said slowly. "She called to tell me that Mr. Hammond had been with her all evening. They weren't at the park when the fireworks went off."

"Lucky for them," Dad said. "Hannah said you were helping the police investigate the accident. Any news?"

"Not so far," I admitted. "But I guess Ms. Waters's call tells me Marcus Hammond had nothing to do with it."

Dad looked surprised. "You thought he did?"

Sitting on the edge of the hall table, I told him the whole story—the details of Mrs. Mahoney's car crash, Charlie's mysterious lights at the battle site, the rock thrown at my car, the phone call diverting the fireworks crew, the canteen filled with cyanide. "Looks like someone's up to no good," Dad agreed, rubbing his jaw. "But why do you think it's Marcus Hammond?"

"Little stuff," I explained. "Like, he seems to go by another name: Martin Halstead. He lives in the same town as the fireworks lady used to. His clothes are all new, like he's traveling incognito. Basically, I just have a bad feeling about him."

Dad didn't look convinced. "Maybe you're inventing evidence because you're afraid Ms. Waters might get her feelings hurt. Anyway, now you know he was with her tonight, so he couldn't have tampered with the fireworks."

"I'm not sure," I said slowly. "Something in her voice seemed odd to me. It's just a hunch, but I'd say she wasn't telling the whole truth."

"Surely you believe Evaline," Dad said, puzzled. "How much more reliable a witness can you have?"

"But, Dad, Ms. Waters is a woman in love. And love makes people act strange sometimes." I sighed. "I'll feel better if I ask Mr. Hammond some questions myself. I keep missing him here at home. I'm going to wait up for him." I fought the impulse to yawn. "He should be in soon."

I turned on the TV and settled into Dad's easy chair while he went to bed. There was a good late-night mystery flick to watch. I figured the sound of Mr. Hammond coming in the front door would wake me up.

I remember the part of the movie where the widow first arrived at the detective's office, but I have no idea how he solved the mystery. The next thing I knew, early morning sunlight was slanting through the blinds, and the phone was ringing. I woke up, groggy. Who would call at this time of the morning? I wondered, stumbling to the phone.

"Oh, Nancy, I hope I didn't wake you."

The familiar voice was like music to my ears.

"*Bess!* No, it's okay, really. You can call anytime, you know that."

"It's just that . . . we've got a problem." Bess's voice wobbled a bit. "I'm out at the battlefield. I came to help the women's auxiliary set up the Union camp hospital. So now we're here going through the supplies . . . and something's wrong."

I was wide awake now. "What, Bess?"

"Well, we have these ceramic jars of salve—a gel that cleans and soothes minor wounds. That's all we expect to treat, scrapes and scratches and all. I opened one jar to see what it looked like, and I smeared some on my finger." She paused.

"Yes?"

"Nancy, it started burning like crazy," Bess said, all in a rush of pent-up worry. "We checked several jars, over and over, and they're all the same: They all burn, and they smell kind of like paint. Nancy, someone's been tampering with our medicine!"

10

Missing in Action

I knew that my plan had been to wait for Marcus Hammond. But Bess's problem was way more urgent. "I'll be right there," I promised. "Call the police."

I wrote a quick note to my dad, asking him to do whatever he could to keep Mr. Hammond at the house until I got back. I slipped into Dad's bedroom and left it on his dresser—no point in letting Mr. Hammond or Hannah read that note. Then I tiptoed to my room, threw on fresh clothes, brushed my teeth, and was back out the door in seven minutes flat.

That time of day the roads were clear, and I made good time to the battlefield site. Pulling in the front entrance, I was amazed at how Charlie's crew had transformed the landscape since Thursday night, building up two boulder-topped ridges that hadn't even been there before. I hardly knew the place, and I'd been hiking in this park since I was a kid.

The parking lot only had a handful of cars in it now, but I suspected it would be overflowing later. The battle wasn't set to begin until 11 A.M., but activity at the site had already begun.

The Union hospital site was near the parking lot, in a log-walled park ranger cabin. Bess was waiting outside, looking stunning in a long pink calico gown with a crisp white apron. She seemed to have forgotten about her darling costume, though. Her face was crumpled with concern.

"Oh, Nancy, it's so good to see you," she cried out, throwing her arms around me in a spontaneous hug. "When we found this stuff, I knew I had to call you. I'm sorry I was so mad the other night—"

"That's over," I said, squeezing her arm. "Not another word about it. We've got a case to solve."

Bess led me inside and showed me a white metal table stacked with rows of thick white ceramic jars, each two inches high and three inches across. I dipped a finger into an open one. It was just as Bess had described—the salve burned to the touch and smelled like pine tar. "Caustic turpentine," I said. "Readily available from any hardware store."

A police officer, consulting in the corner with the

head nurse on duty, spoke up. "That's my guess too. We'll send a sample to the lab to make sure."

"Could it be lethal?" Bess asked, her blue eyes widening.

"Lethal? Not when you apply it externally," I said. "A bad skin irritation would be the worst."

Bess let out a sigh of relief. "So whoever did this is no killer."

"I wouldn't go that far," I said. "Granted, we couldn't be killed with this, but who knows what other trouble the culprit may be up to." I filled Bess in on all the developments she had missed.

"Whoa, Nancy. I don't talk to you for two days and you get up to all kinds of trouble," Bess said with a wistful smile.

"I could have used your help," I admitted.

"Well, you've got it now," she said firmly.

To keep myself from getting weepy, I hurried back to the problem at hand. "Just where did this salve come from?" I asked.

The head nurse heard my question and joined us. "We got it from a medical supply house; it comes in big gallon-size drums. It's a product I use all the time down at River Heights General. We just put it into these old-fashioned jars to look authentic."

"I checked the ointment that's still in the drum," Bess said. "It seems to be fine."

"How many people do you have working here?" I asked, glancing around.

"There are only six on the early shift," the nurse said, "but there were twenty-five or so yesterday afternoon, when we filled the pots with salve. Right, Bess?"

Bess nodded. "There was lots to do—everyone was busy. No one was watching anybody else very closely."

"I gave the police officer a list of who all was here at the time," the nurse said. "I assume they'll be questioned."

"I came as soon as I heard," Mrs. Mahoney's voice sang out from the doorway. "This is the last straw. All that fuss at the picnic grounds last night, and now this!" She bustled in, wearing a vintage gown of dove-gray wool. She may have been distraught, but Mrs. Mahoney had made sure she was perfectly dressed before coming out.

I knew Mrs. Mahoney had been in River Heights General the previous afternoon, but I spent a few minutes questioning her about the different people who'd had access to the salve.

Then, out of the corner of my eye, I saw Evaline Waters edge through the doorway. Her costume was a drab brown striped cotton dress, probably the most like a real nurse's outfit of the time.

"Evaline, dear," Mrs. Mahoney called out, "you were here yesterday. Come tell Nancy what you saw."

Ms. Waters shot me a terrified look. That really shook me. I had known Ms. Waters most of my life—why would she be scared of me?

"I wasn't in charge of that job," she said, eyes not meeting mine. "But I did see Nathan Emory show up, bringing the little white crocks."

"Nathan Emory?" I said, startled.

"Yes, he brought a whole box full of them," Bess explained.

"He informed me a few days ago that he had a number of vintage medicine crocks on hand," Mrs. Mahoney added. I doubted just how "vintage" those jars really were, but I didn't mention that. "I thought they'd make a splendid period detail for the hospital," she went on, "so I ordered them. I think I still have his business card somewhere."

She took from her purse a small ivory-colored square of cardboard, printed with the name "Emory's Armory." I glanced at it hurriedly, and then something caught my eye. "Potsdam, New York?" I read, shocked. I glanced at Evaline Waters. She had gone totally pale. Obviously she recognized the name as Hammond's current hometown.

"What's all this about?" Mrs. Mahoney demanded. "Nathan Emory is quite a specialist in the Civil War, you know. Surely you can't suspect him of this tampering."

"Mrs. Mahoney, remember the canteen Mr. Emory gave you last night?" I said. "Was it empty when he gave it to you?"

Mrs. Mahoney looked puzzled. "Why, yes, it seemed to be. I didn't hold it for long, though. Evaline, was that canteen I gave you empty?"

Evaline looked paler than ever. "Yes, it was—when you gave it to me."

"Why do you ask, Nancy?" Mrs. Mahoney demanded.

I faced the two older women squarely. "Because we found the canteen later at the picnic grounds—filled with water laced with cyanide."

Ms. Waters and Bess gasped. Mrs. Mahoney raised her eyebrows. "Had anyone drunk from it?" she asked.

"As far as we know, only one poor stray cat," I replied.

Just then the police officer drew Mrs. Mahoney over to ask some questions. Evaline Waters tugged at my sleeve. Her voice faltered. "Nancy . . . you know, Marcus was here at the hospital yesterday too." Her dark eyes met mine steadily now.

"Was he putting the salve into the jars?" I asked gently. She nodded, eyes filling with tears.

I sighed. "Nathan Emory is from Potsdam. Isn't that where Mr. Hammond lives too?"

She nodded. "I believe they've met."

"Yes," I said, choosing my words carefully, "but Nathan Emory seems to know Mr. Hammond by a different name—Martin Halstead."

Ms. Waters bit her lip and shrugged. "I—I don't know about that," she said faintly.

I reached out and took her two hands in mine. "Who is Marcus Hammond, really?" I asked.

She hesitated, then gave Bess and me a pleading gaze. "Marcus? I've known him for years, girls. Or rather, I knew him years ago—twenty-five years ago. He only lived in River Heights for a year or so. We dated for six months." Her eyes misted over. "He was charming, sensitive, funny. I guess you could call it a whirlwind romance. But then . . ."

"Then?" I urged her on.

"Marcus had a small construction firm. And Mr. Mahoney—that mean, ruthless man—drove him out of business. I told Marcus he should build a new business, but he was so bitter, he left town in a huff. He barely said good-bye. He promised to send me his address once he was settled, but he never did. It was as if he had vanished from the earth."

Bess's eyes filled with sympathetic tears. "That must have been awful! What did you do?"

Ms. Waters shrugged. "I waited awhile, but . . . well, life went on. I had my friends, my house, my

109

career. I stopped thinking about Marcus Hammond."

"Until—," I prodded her.

She sighed. "One day out of the blue, last April, I got a flyer about his new venture, this online genealogy search. I e-mailed him, wondering if it was the same Marcus Hammond. He suggested that if River Heights staged a reenactment, he might get business and then he could come visit. The idea stirred up old memories. I started researching the Civil War to find a battle we could reenact."

"And the rest is history," Bess said, a dreamy look on her face. She was swept up in the romance.

But I had more practical things on my mind. "When Marcus finally showed up, did he seem like the same guy you'd known long ago?" I asked.

Ms. Waters flinched. "Yes—and no. He could still be charming. But whenever he heard anything about the Mahoneys, he overreacted. He insisted I communicate with the historical society, so he wouldn't have to talk to Mrs. Mahoney. And then, when he showed up last Wednesday, he gave me that information about Josiah Mahoney being a deserter. He insisted I make it public."

"To embarrass Mrs. Mahoney," Bess said.

Ms. Waters lowered her voice. "Marcus hoped to neutralize Mrs. Mahoney, to make it easier for him to operate in River Heights. I went along with it. I was a little miffed myself—I'd done all the Black Creek research, and she took all the credit."

"Yesterday she was very gracious about that," I reminded Ms. Waters.

She wrung her hands. "Marcus filled my ears with his view of things," she fretted. "And he paid me so much attention, it turned my head." She gazed off into the distance. "These past few days have been thrilling, Nancy, I'll admit. But last night he pushed me too far. He demanded I lie to you."

I raised my eyebrows. "He really wasn't with you all evening?"

She shook her head no. "After Mrs. Mahoney gave me that canteen, he acted upset, took it away from me, and insisted that we leave the picnic. He dropped me at my house and drove away. I was so hurt; I went for a long walk. When I came back, Marcus was waiting outside. He told me I had to call you and give him an alibi."

"He used that word, *alibi*?" Bess asked.

Ms. Waters squeezed her eyes shut. "I did it. But the rest of the night I couldn't sleep. All I could think of was how his hatred of the Mahoneys had twisted him." She opened her eyes. They glittered with brave tears. "When I heard all this stuff this morning—about the tampered salve, the poisoned canteen, Marcus having a second name—I realized he's not the man I thought he was. And if he's up to no good, Nancy, I'll help you catch him!"

I left Bess with her arm around Ms. Waters while I went outside with my cell phone to call home. I saw that the parking lot was more than half full by now. Dozens of people in uniform roamed around on the grass, getting psyched for the battle.

Finally Dad answered the phone. "Dad," I said, "is Mr. Hammond still there?"

Dad paused. "Nancy, I'm sorry," he said. "I got your note. But when I went down the hall to catch Hammond, he'd already left."

My heart jumped. "Left?"

"Apparently he cleared out yesterday afternoon, before the picnic. Took everything with him. All he left was a typed note."

"Save that note for the police, Dad," I said. "I think we've got our man."

An hour later I met Chief McGinnis outside the Union hospital. "But, Chief McGinnis," I pleaded, "Marcus Hammond has endangered several lives already. Just because no one has been seriously harmed yet—"

"We don't know for a fact that he did any of these things," the chief reminded me. "Look, I'm willing to put out an all-points bulletin on the guy. My men will stop him before he can skip town. But I refuse to postpone the reenactment. Too many people have planned too long to disappoint them."

"I'm not asking you to cancel it. Just start it later, so you can make it more secure," I begged.

The chief gave me his most withering look. "We've got security in place, Miss Drew," he said. "The reenactment starts in one hour. Now good-bye." He wheeled and walked back to his waiting car.

I hate it when he calls me Miss Drew!

"The reenactment starts in one hour," Deirdre Shannon whined, hurrying toward me. "And you're not even dressed."

I turned to look at Deirdre. She had, in the end, gone for the butternut uniform. It did go well with her black hair. And she'd evidently paid extra for someone to tailor the baggy trousers and shapeless coat until they clung to the curves of her body.

I was just about to tell her that I was skipping the battle when my better sense kicked in. If Chief McGinnis wouldn't call off the battle, then our saboteur was still at large. Where better to head him off than on the battlefield itself?

"My uniform's in my car," I said, remembering that it had been in my trunk ever since I'd rented it on Thursday. I'd been so busy, I'd completely forgotten about it until now. "Where can I change?"

My gray uniform—a typical rental—was wrinkled and baggy and not nearly as flattering as Deirdre's. But that hardly mattered. As soon as I came out of the canvas tent, I took stock of my surroundings. I remembered the plan to plant explosives near the ammunition storage—that would be a ripe spot for mayhem. "Where's the Confederate arsenal?" I asked Deirdre.

She pointed up a slope to the edge of the woods. "Up there. Let's go rent our weapons. I'd like a long silver sword. That would look awesome hanging down my side, wouldn't it?" She posed, as if she was on a catwalk.

"You can't have a saber if you're not in the cavalry, Deirdre," I explained. "And you can't be in the cavalry if you don't have a horse." I managed to swallow my annoyance as we went up the slope. With George and Bess stationed elsewhere, and Ned being a pacifist, I needed an ally in the field and, like it or not, Deirdre was my best option.

The arsenal was a long, windowless wood shed with bins of rifles to rent for the day. It seemed like a hundred folks in Confederate costume were trailing in and out, arming themselves. I picked out a rifle—a cheap, scarred replica, way inferior to the beautiful things Nathan Emory sold. Stepping away from the bins, I practiced sighting along its tin barrel and thrusting with its wobbly, dull bayonet. Not much danger of hurting the enemy with this toy.

"Weird. What's this?" I heard Deirdre say.

I found her at the back of the shed, where a stack of dull tin swords had been left. Two small, flat, unmarked wooden crates were tucked into the corner under a canvas sheet, as if intentionally hidden away.

Deirdre and I stared at the mysterious boxes. "Wonder what's in them," I said. I leaned over and pried up the wooden lid.

Bullets—lumpy lead bullets, dully gleaming in ordered rows. Real bullets.

In a half-empty box.

11

The Real Deal

Are those real bullets?" Deirdre said, confused. "I thought this was a safe reenactment—no bullets allowed."

"That's right," I said. "Someone must have smuggled these in."

"But why?" she asked.

Deirdre wasn't too swift.

"If he puts real bullets in his gun," I said, "and he's fighting as a Confederate, he can shoot Union reenactors. They won't have bullets, so they can't shoot him back. And then they'll go, wounded, to the Union hospital, where a nurse will put salve on their wounds—a salve that turns out to be even more dangerous. It's an ideal plan, really. You don't even have to be a good shot to do serious damage."

Deirdre's eyes grew wide. "But why would they use dangerous salve at the Union hospital?"

"Because somebody—and I bet it's the same person—snuck it into their supplies," I explained. "Bess discovered it there this morning."

"So now we're safe," Deirdre said, relaxing.

"Well, the hospital part of this scheme may have been foiled," I said, "but we're not safe yet, not by any means. Not if this madman's running around with half a crate of bullets, ready to fire them at innocent reenactors."

Deirdre nodded. "Right. And what if it's more than one person? There could be someone on the Union side who's in on the same plot."

My heart sank. I had been fixed on the idea of one saboteur, someone who was taking sides too personally in this battle. But Deirdre was right. What if it was a widespread scheme?

"Let's do what we can do to stop them, then," I declared. "Could you take a handful of these bullets to show Chief McGinnis, DeeDee? Maybe that will convince him to postpone the battle."

I realized I had slipped and used Deirdre's old nickname. But for once, she didn't react. She actually seemed set on helping me. First Bess and George and I get into a fight, and now Deirdre is acting a little friendly! What next?

We immediately showed the outfitter running the weapon rentals what we'd found. The shocked look on his face told me that the boxes of bullets were news to him. He quickly ordered them to be taken away. Deirdre went to find the police chief, while I questioned the arsenal staff.

The sentry in charge told me he had opened the doors at nine this morning, but he swore the arsenal was locked from eight o'clock last night until he opened up. Other workers said they were positive there had been nothing in that corner late yesterday afternoon. But when I questioned them more closely, no one could say for sure that it had still been empty at the end of the day, when the shed was locked.

I took a look at the lock. As I'd suspected, it wasn't a supersecure device—just a combination padlock with a stout hasp. This was only a temporary site, after all, and there had been nothing of much value to protect in the shed. When I tilted the padlock, I could see a few scratches in the chrome.

"Someone messed with this lock," I said. "If he or she was able to pick it, the lock could have been opened and then relocked. Someone could have gotten in last night to hide these bullets here."

In my mind I went over the time frame we were considering. Nathan Emory had no alibi between eight o'clock, when the canteen was presented to Mrs. Mahoney, and ten, when the police brought Nathan Emory to the picnic site. And no one had seen Marcus Hammond anytime after eight until he showed up at Evaline's later on. That left him plenty of time to break into the arsenal and hide a box of illegal bullets.

Walking back down the slope from the arsenal, I reached into my pocket for my cell phone, then remembered: The organizers had asked reenactors not to bring such modern devices to the field. Smart idea. How authentic could a battle seem when your enemy suddenly stops and whips out a wireless phone? But now I felt at a loss. Surely if one person could break the rules by smuggling in real bullets, I could break the rules by having a harmless cell phone. Without it, I just had to sit by the arsenal and wait for Deirdre to show up, hopefully with a cooperative Chief McGinnis. Not very promising.

By now the site was getting crowded. The parking lot was stuffed with cars, and a field across from the entrance had been commandeered to hold even more. The pathways from the parking lot were a blend of Union blue and rebel gray and butternut, folks chatting and trading jokes. But where the pathways branched off, at a row of trash bins, blue sorted from the others. The "soldiers" lowered their heads and began to turn serious, getting into their parts.

Some of the sutlers had set up their booths on the grassy verge of the parking lot. I spotted the sign for Emory's Armory. Like he'd said, battle day was his big moneymaker, and there was a line in front of his booth. No doubt folks had decided to buy their own rifles once they saw what the rentals were like. I knew that most of them would be frustrated by the twenty-four-hour waiting period for a permit to own a gun, as opposed to rentals equipped only with blanks. Thank goodness there are laws like that to keep guns out of the wrong hands, but gun control laws aren't foolproof. I assumed the police had already questioned Emory about the medicine crocks, but it wouldn't hurt to follow up. I sauntered toward his booth. He saw me coming over the heads of browsing customers. The way he stiffened up told me that I wasn't exactly welcome. But when did I ever let something like that stop me?

"Mr. Emory," I called out, "did you hear about the problem at the hospital this morning?"

"I already talked to the police," Emory grumbled. "Those jars were clean when I delivered them. You have my word for that. That'll be one hundred eighty-five," he said to a buyer. "And I'll need to see a picture ID and a copy of your gun permit. Yes, I accept credit cards."

I stepped around the side of his booth to continue our conversation while he ran the man's credit card through his machine. "Then what about these?" I pulled one of the bullets we'd found out of my pocket and showed it to him.

Emory glanced sideways, irritated at first. But he didn't hide his startled reaction when he saw the bullet. "Where'd that come from?" he asked.

"It looks to me like an item you were selling the first day of the bazaar," I pointed out. "Until the organizers told you not to."

Emory handed the credit card slip to his customer to sign. "I didn't like them slapping my hand about that," he admitted. "I figure people know they're not supposed to use real ammo in a reenactment; it's not up to the vendor to keep bullets away from them. But I took the minnie balls out of my display, like they asked."

Now it was my turn to be startled. "Minnie balls?"

"Sure, that's what those are called," Emory said. "They were the first bullets developed for rifles. The old muskets still used round bullets, you see." He took the bullet from me and held it up to demonstrate. "These bullets were more oblong, with a flat base, so they fit snugly inside a rifle's grooved barrel. That made them fly more accurately toward their target. They were twice as deadly as musket balls—a big innovation." He handed the bullet back to me with a satisfied sniff.

I had to admit, he knew his stuff. Now if I could just remember when I'd heard someone mention minnie balls before.

"It's not too hard for someone to buy minnie balls," Emory said, separating the credit card copies and handing one back to his buyer. "There's no way to trace the source for those. I didn't sell any at the bazaar." He paused for a moment. "Okay," he said, lowering his voice, "so I did sell a couple of boxes privately. So what?"

That's when it hit me. Nathan Emory sold minnie balls out of his trunk. "You sold them to Marcus Hammond!"

Emory frowned. "Hammond? No. I sold some to Martin Halstead, a guy I know from home. I figured he knew the reenactment rules. He told me they were for his own private use, for target practice in his backyard. . . ." Emory's voice trailed off as he saw the look on my face. "Where did you get those, though?"

"They were in the Confederate arsenal this morning," I said in a low voice, hoping not to scare any bystanders. "We hid them away, but one crate was already half empty."

Emory gave me all of his attention now. "I sold him two full crates," he said.

I blew out a sigh. "You say you know Hammond—er, Halstead—from home?"

Emory nodded. "From Potsdam. But not very well. He came to my shop last April or so, asking for information about reenactments."

"April?" That was when he'd first mentioned the reenactment idea to Evaline Waters, I recalled.

Emory nodded. "He was the first one who clued me in about this River Heights deal. The way he talked, I figured he was one of the organizers. I figured I could trust him."

"Well, he isn't one of the organizers, and apparently you can't trust him," I said.

Emory screwed his hands into fists. "Where is he now? I'm gonna let him have it. Putting my reputation on the line—"

"We don't know where he is," I said. "The police are looking for him. I wondered if you had any leads on his whereabouts."

Emory shook his head. "I heard he was staying with a family in town, but I don't know where."

At that, I winced. Hammond had been right under my nose, and I hadn't been able to stop him!

"I couldn't even tell you what kind of car he drives," Emory went on. "But if I see him, I'll bring him down, believe me. These reenactments are my bread and butter. If one turns deadly, the whole business will be shut down. I can't afford that."

For once, I felt I could rely on Nathan Emory. I gave him a police number to call if he did see Hammond. Then I set out again on my search.

I remembered Hammond saying he was enrolled in the Fourth Mississippi Regiment. I checked the battlefield map that was being handed out at the entrance. That regiment's headquarters was at the foot of the slope by the arsenal, so I headed that way.

Entering the Fourth Mississippi's camp area, I saw dozens of soldiers in butternut and gray among the canvas tents, examining rifles, filling canteens, cooking bacon, and toasting bread on long forks over little campfires. The scene looked like a total time warp, until you looked closely and saw that the pieces of bread they were toasting were halves of modern bagels.

"Nancy?" A voice behind me made me jump. I turned around to see Todd Willetts, buttoning on a gray uniform jacket.

"Todd!" I said, surprised. "Is this the Confederate regiment you're leading?"

He shrugged. "The organizers owe me one," he said, fiddling uneasily with the yellow braid on his gray sleeves. "Now that I've put on this uniform, I feel like a turncoat—literally. It'll sure feel weird to shoot against boys in blue."

"I'm glad to see you," I said. "I'm looking for a guy in this regiment—Marcus Hammond. He also goes by Martin Halstead. You said you knew him."

Todd frowned. "Halstead—the family tree guy? Yeah, I met him before, at another reenactment. I saw him at the bazaar a couple of times, but he never came to any of our regiment's meetings or drills. Let me check." He picked up a clipboard and leafed through some papers. "He's not on my list, under either name. You sure he's signed up?"

"I'm not sure of anything about him anymore," I said, suddenly feeling very tired. "He could be anywhere on the battlefield, I guess." I checked my watch. "Lucky it's only nine thirty."

"Nine thirty?" Todd shook his head, pulling out an antique silver pocket watch. He flipped open the lid and showed me the face. "It's ten forty-five."

Oops. Served me right for being so attached to my mom's old watch. It was always stopping on me. But if it was ten forty-five, then time was really running out!

"Good luck finding Martin. Once the battle starts, it'll be chaos around here," Todd went on. "If I see him, I'll say you're looking for him."

"If you see him," I said, "grab him and turn him in to the police. We think he may have live bullets in his gun, and reason to use them."

Todd clenched his fists, looking outraged at the very idea. "I won't let him get away with that," he promised. "Sorry, but I have to line up my troops now. I'll keep an eye open."

Thanking Todd, I jogged away. It seemed that the surest way I could catch Hammond was to get as many people as possible involved. By now I had Bess, Nathan Emory, and Todd Willetts on the lookout. But it would help to have someone on the Union side—and that meant George.

I checked my map to find the Twelfth Michigan Regiment's camp. It was on the far side of the park, near the river bluffs. I would have time to cross the battle site safely before the reenactment got under way. I began to jog up the slope.

I was barely fifty yards away from Todd's tent when a cannon boom echoed off the rocky ledges nearby. I spun around to see what was happening.

I heard Todd Willetts shout, "Battle ho!" A second later another commander near him called out "Battle ho!" too.

With a low murmur the half-organized lines of soldiers began to fall into step, still strapping on their gear pouches.

The battle had begun—ten minutes ahead of schedule!

12

No Stopping Now

I was far enough up the slope to see several regiments in their campsites, hurrying into battle formation. No one questioned whether it was an official start. They were too busy scrambling to join in.

I checked my watch but, as usual, it had stopped. I couldn't be sure, but it seemed a good bet that the signal to begin the battle had come early. That was why the troops looked so disorganized. At this point, though, I didn't see who would stop them.

I began to run hard. If I was going to cross the Union line and find George before the shooting started, I'd have to hustle!

I burst through the woods and over the crest of the first ridge. Soon I was looking down into a steeply sided valley with a creek running down the middle. Charlie and his friends had dug that two days before to make it look like Black Creek. Most of the hand-to-hand fighting would take place there.

I couldn't see any Union soldiers yet, but I suspected several of them would be hiding behind the boulders on the ridge opposite. Those rocks were perfect spots for sharpshooters to hide and pick off enemies as they came over the ridge.

Scoping out the landscape, I felt sorry for the Confederates. Advancing up that ridge, they would be sitting ducks. It was no easy thing to face a hilltop full of snipers, even when you believed they only had blanks in their guns. The original soldiers, though, had been facing live bullets. That really took guts.

And if my suspicions were correct, today's soldiers might be facing live bullets too!

Suddenly I saw a knot of people running up the valley, along the fake creek. Chief McGinnis, bullhorn in hand, was in front. Behind him it looked like Pam Mattei and her pyrotechnical crew, all wearing hard hats, were trying to catch up.

McGinnis raised the bullhorn. His voice blared out, "Stop your marching! That wasn't the signal! Troops, halt!"

His amplified voice bounced off the sides of the valley. But even at the top of the ridge, it sounded tinny and far away. There was no way the soldiers on the other side of the ridge would hear it above the stamp of marching feet and repeated cannon booms. It was far too late to call off this battle now.

I began to run down the steep valley wall, leaping recklessly from rock to rock. I had to reach the chief!

I saw Pam Mattei grab his arm and begin arguing with him. As I drew nearer I heard her saying, ". . . all on a timing system. If we stop this thing and start again, the explosions will go off too soon. The battle choreography was all worked out ahead of time. If it gets thrown off, troops might be standing right there when it blows."

Behind her, her crew chief, Wilson, added, "We can't reset the charges now. We're using underground fuses; they've already been lighted."

The chief, looking distracted, caught sight of me and whirled around. "Nancy, Deirdre showed me the bullets. You were right. We should stop this thing immediately." The look he flashed me was the closest I'd ever seen him come to an apology.

"Someone fired a rogue cannon," Wilson sputtered. "It wasn't the designated cannon, but who could tell? Someone started the battle early, for whatever reason. There's no turning back now."

At that moment a blank shot happened to whistle

past the chief's ear. He flinched, his eyes wide and scared. Even with a trained policeman's instincts, he seemed really thrown by all this.

I peered up the rocky ridge, spotting a few rifle barrels poking over and around the boulders. "I have to get to the Union side, Chief. We need to spread the word to catch Marcus Hammond."

"Marcus Hammond?" Pam Mattei grabbed my arm. "Do you know where he is?"

I didn't want to show my hand yet—I still wasn't sure how Mattei was involved. "Do you know him?" I shouted over the growing battle noises. "From Potsdam?"

Mattei pulled on the chief's sleeve and yelled into his ear. "This Halstead guy I'm after—Hammond seems to be his alias here."

"You're after him?" I asked, confused.

"Ms. Mattei is undercover with the FBI," the chief told me. "Or so I learned last night." From his tone of voice, I guessed he was peeved that she hadn't informed local authorities sooner.

"Not many people know what Hammond looks like, Chief," I shouted back. "Everyone who does should be alerted. We can't arrest just any man with glasses and curly gray hair. I have to find my friend George and get her help. I think she's seen him and knows what he looks like." Even as I said that, I searched my memory. Had George been with me any of the times I'd encountered Marcus Hammond?

"And go to the Union side?" the chief asked. "But you're wearing a rebel uniform—you'll be shot."

"They're only shooting blanks," I argued.

The chief looked grim. "And what if one of those sharpshooters is Marcus Hammond?"

I clenched my jaw. "I'll run fast and low."

The chief shook his head. "I should know better than to try to stop you, Nancy," he gave in. "Go ahead. But be extremely careful. We'll do what we can from here, right, Ms. Mattei?"

She nodded. "Nancy," Ms. Mattei warned, "Chief McGinnis is right. Be very careful."

With that, I took off. I jumped over the narrow creek and, crouching low, started to work my way up the ridge. A wave of rebs were coming over the ridgetop now. The Union rifles were trained in that direction. Hopefully they wouldn't notice me.

I dodged from bush to tree to bush, keeping south of the fighting. My mind was totally focused on Marcus Hammond. Pam Mattei was cleared of suspicion now, and so was Nathan Emory. That left one suspect with no alibi and plenty of opportunity to commit these crimes—Hammond. I still couldn't figure out his motive, but that could be cleared up later, once we had him in police custody.

Within three minutes I came up under the lip of a patch of boulders. Grabbing hold of one of them, I saw with surprise that it wasn't a real rock, but cast concrete. Charlie's crew had done an amazing job. I swung myself up into a narrow crevice between two boulders. I could just fit through.

Behind the boulders, I looked north and saw a line of Union sharpshooters, kneeling or lying on their stomachs, pointing their rifles down the ridge. Farther down the ridge six or seven cannons were set up, pointing over the hilltop. Each had a crew of six scurrying around, loading charges into the cannon mouth.

The nearest sharpshooter, a heavyset young guy, saw me out of the corner of his eye. He jerked around, looking scared. I raised my hands to show him that I didn't have my rifle. He pointed his gun at me anyway and pulled the trigger. I heard a sharp crack and saw a little puff of powder smoke come out of the barrel.

I waved and ran on. Behind me I heard the guy shout, "Hey, you're supposed to fall down!"

I started to skitter and slide down the far side of the ridge. Ahead of me a line of barbed wire gleamed in the sunlight, cutting off my path. I flattened onto my stomach to squirm under it.

As I wriggled I felt the jacket of my uniform tug hard, caught on the barbed wire. The rough gray cloth ripped loudly. "Darn it!" I muttered. I jerked one arm out of the coat, then the other. It would be quicker to leave it behind, and probably safer, too. Dressed in my white T-shirt and gray pants, I wasn't so obviously marked as a Confederate.

Downhill, though, I saw a tangle of dark blue Union uniforms coming toward me, rifles in hand. I ducked behind a patch of shrubs.

It was one thing to imagine the battle landscape when Charlie described it to me. Now it looked totally different. There were people everywhere, milling around, shouting, waving guns. Cannons had begun shooting continuously, filling the air with a haze of gray powder.

I could barely think straight with all the noise and confusion. So this was what war was like, I thought. A big smoky mess.

By now I could barely see three feet ahead of me. But there, miraculously, in the mass of charging blue uniforms, I saw George. Her short dark hair was tucked up under a flat cap, and her blue jacket and trousers were way baggy, but I'd know that slim athletic build anywhere. I flung myself toward her. "George!" I yelled.

She pulled back, surprised, lowering her rifle. "Nancy?" She looked like she didn't know whether or not to smile. I guessed Bess hadn't had time to tell her we'd made up.

Then George gave in and grinned. That girl never can hold a grudge. Her arms opened to give me a hug. "What are you doing, Nancy—deserting to the Union?"

I quickly hugged her back. "George, you've got to help," I shouted. "There's a saboteur running around. We've got to catch him before—"

Suddenly, in a pause between cannon blasts, the air cleared. I heard hoofbeats and a shrill horse's whinny. I stared downhill past George.

A large gray horse was prancing along the flat grassy area at the bottom of the hill, just behind the battle lines. The man riding him was big and burly, with an officer's slouch hat on his head. From his swaggering posture, I felt sure it was Art Jeffries.

Something—I don't know, call it intuition—made me look uphill. From here we could only see the backs of the sharpshooters, facing away from us as they pointed their guns downhill toward the advancing rebs.

Except for one.

Outlined on the ridge, one Union sharpshooter was turned facing us. Down on one knee, he raised his rifle, steadying it on his shoulder. He lowered his face to peer along the barrel. The sun glinted off his glasses, and gray curls poked out from under his cap.

Swiftly, he took aim at Art Jeffries.

13

Heat of Battle

I heard a scream, but soon I realized that it was coming from me. I also realized that it was pointless. No one except George was going to hear me in this insane mess!

I grabbed a fake revolver I saw on the ground and threw it with all my might uphill toward the shooter—unmistakably Hammond. As it flew toward him he saw it out of the corner of his eye and jerked aside. It was just enough to throw off his shot. The bullet shot up into the sky instead of downhill.

Meanwhile George had started running down the slope toward Jeffries and his horse. "Colonel Jeffries!" she yelled, straining her voice to rise over the battle.

I didn't wait to see if George could pull Jeffries to safety. I was too busy getting up the ridge to Hammond. He saw me now. Clutching his rifle, he spun around and began to climb the boulders to get away from me.

Just then the advancing rebel line broke over the top. Undaunted by the Union sharpshooters, they'd fought their way over the ridge. Rifles were lowered and bayonets pointed as the two sides clashed in hand-to-hand combat.

The wave of soldiers pushed Hammond backward. I heard a fellow Union reenactor yell to him, "Hey, you were using live ammo—that smoke didn't come from blanks!" The Union soldier grabbed Hammond by the shoulder and jerked him backward. Two other reenactors, hearing the accusation, furiously dropped their rifles, jumped on top of Hammond, and wrestled him to the ground.

Hammond may have been fit for his age, but he was outnumbered. By the time I reached him, he had stopped struggling and was trying to put his broken glasses back on. He glared at me. "Why don't you mind your own business?" he snarled.

Before I could answer, one of the reenactors, his voice choking with outrage, told Hammond, "You break the rules, we take you down." He yanked the loaded rifle out of Hammond's hands. "Come on, buddy. It's court-martial time."

I followed as the soldiers marched Hammond

downhill to a large canvas tent. Art Jeffries was sitting inside on a wooden crate, his slouch hat on a folding camp desk beside him. He looked sweaty and upset. He jumped when the soldiers shoved Hammond, head hanging low, through the tent flap.

"This guy broke the rules," one of the soldiers announced, giving Hammond an angry push.

I stepped forward with Hammond's rifle. "Look, Mr. Jeffries." I broke open the barrel and shook the gun. Two live bullets fell on the ground.

Jeffries went pale for a second, but he quickly got his swagger back. "What's this all about, soldier?"

Hammond raised his head slowly. Seeing his face, Jeffries jumped again, startled. "Marcus Hammond—the same one who used to live here in River Heights? Why, I haven't thought of you in twenty years. What're you doing around here again?"

"More fried chicken, girls?" Hannah offered, bringing in a second loaded platter. It was Sunday night, and we were having a sort of reunion dinner—me, George, and Bess—along with Dad, Hannah, Ned, Ms. Waters, and Harold Safer.

"Ooh, Hannah, yes, please. I just love your fried chicken," Bess said, licking her fingers.

"But, Bess, it's *Southern* fried chicken," my dad teased.

Bess flushed, but she kept her cool. "I'm learning to be open-minded, Mr. Drew."

"So, Nancy, did Chief McGinnis fill you in on the outcome of the case yet?" Dad asked me, pouring himself some more lemonade.

"Mr. Hammond made a full confession," I said. "It looks like a classic case of someone starting out with little lies, then doing bad things to cover them up until the whole thing got out of hand. When he set out, he just wanted to use an old friend—Ms. Waters—to drum up business."

"But he already had his online genealogy operation, didn't he?" George asked.

I hesitated. "Well, yes and no. It was really just a scam. People sent him money, and he sent them trumped-up family trees. It wasn't doing so well; too many legitimate businesses competing with it. He thought a reenactment would suck in some new clients."

"It sure did," Bess said. "It seemed like everybody in town used his site."

"That was the problem," I explained, buttering one of Hannah's yummy buttermilk biscuits. "He didn't count on getting so many search requests from River Heights. He couldn't keep up with the volume, so he started repeating himself."

Dad nodded. "That's why so many people believed

they had ancestors in the Seventh Illinois Regiment."

"Exactly. But then he started to feel the heat. Pam Mattei showed up in Potsdam and started nosing around."

"That fireworks woman?" Bess said, surprised.

I nodded. "An FBI agent, it turns out, assigned to check out Internet scams. Though Hammond's operation was pretty small potatoes, it was part of a larger ongoing investigation, so she felt it was worth her time to sniff him out. Hammond decided he'd better come to River Heights to cover his tracks. Mattei followed him. Dawn's Early Light was just her cover."

"That explains why she didn't know much about pyrotechnics," Harold added from his end of the table. "She had me fooled at first. But then, I don't know anything about fireworks either!"

"So *that's* why he was so touchy, even before he arrived," Evaline Waters added. "He was already under the gun. When Agnes Mahoney wrote to him, questioning his research, he reacted very badly." She looked down, as if embarrassed. "I guess that should've tipped me off."

"You couldn't have known his research was bogus," Bess said.

"I should've spotted that. I *am* a librarian, after all," Ms. Waters said firmly. "But I also should have remembered Marcus's old grudge against Art Jeffries and Mrs. Mahoney. That's what really got him into trouble."

"He does seem obsessed with them," I agreed. "What happened all those years ago?"

Ms. Waters sighed, crumbling a biscuit. "I already told you that Mr. Mahoney drove Marcus out of business," she said. "But I didn't tell you why. See, Art Jeffries worked for the Mahoneys back then. He was their chauffeur. Marcus was doing a little construction job on the Mahoney property. One day he caught Art siphoning gas from the Mahoney's limo and threatened to turn him in. Then Art caught Marcus using shoddy materials, and tried to blackmail him into keeping quiet about the gas."

"So both of them were guilty," Dad said.

Ms. Waters nodded. "Finally they both went to Agnes Mahoney to rat each other out. She sided with Art Jeffries. He was her full-time employee, after all, and he's always been good at buttering up important people. Anyway, she told the late Mr. Mahoney that Marcus was cutting corners on the job. Mr. Mahoney used that information to ruin Marcus's business. I didn't know this at the time, I only saw that Marcus was gloomy and preoccupied. The night before he left, he told me the whole story."

"So all these years he was waiting for revenge?" George said.

"Not really," Evaline said. "But once he got that letter from Mrs. Mahoney, it all flooded back. You should have seen the gleeful look on his face when he gave me that research about Josiah Mahoney."

"Do you think he made that up?" George asked.

She nodded. "Most likely he did, just to humiliate Agnes."

"Then he got the idea of tampering with her brakes," I went on. "Throwing the wrench he used into Art Jeffries's car afterward was just a spur-of-the-moment act to implicate Jeffries—a way of hurting both of them at once."

"What about the rock through your windshield?" my father asked. "Did he do that? That couldn't have affected Jeffries or Mrs. Mahoney."

"He admitted doing that, too," I said. "He said he followed Pam Mattei out to the battlefield site Thursday night, getting nervous about what she knew. He was still there when Charlie Adams showed up, so he hid, hoping not to be spotted. When he heard Charlie call me on his cell phone, he got worried that I was on to him too. That's why he threw the rock through my windshield—to scare me off."

"Not that it ever works," Ned said, grinning.

"And the fireworks? I assume that was him?" Harold asked. I knew he was still annoyed that someone had ruined his picnic.

I nodded. "His fingerprints matched those on the computer controls. And it was his cell phone number that called Wilson with the fake car alarm report, to draw the crew off the barge."

"Which just proves he's not a professional criminal," Ms. Waters pointed out. I think a part of her still wanted to defend her old flame. "He left clues all over the place."

"Well, he thought he was safe," I pointed out. "He knew there were no fingerprints on any police file for him. He didn't know I'd taken prints from his room here. And the cell phone, that was in Martin Halstead's name. So he thought no one could tie him to the fireworks sabotage."

"He forgot that people like Nathan Emory and Todd Willetts would be in town for the reenactment," Dad said. "People who could identify him as Martin Halstead."

"Apparently he started using that name about ten years ago, after he almost got caught in another business scam," I explained.

"What about the cyanide in the canteen?" Ms. Waters asked next, with a sad look in her eyes. "Did he put that there to . . . to harm me?"

"That was another thing he made up as he went along," I said. "He had cyanide with him, hoping to slip it into Art Jeffries's drink. Then Jeffries didn't come to the picnic—but suddenly Mrs. Mahoney was there. And when he saw Emory give her the canteen, he smelled an opportunity. But before he could slip in the poison, she gave it to you instead, Ms. Waters."

"So that's why he seemed upset," she mused. "And here I thought it was just because he didn't want me getting credit for the reenactment."

"He took it away from you and got you away from the picnic," I said. "But he put the cyanide in the canteen anyway before he left. By that point, he just wanted to mess up the reenactment events as much as possible. He says he figured that would keep people too busy to notice their fake genealogies, at the same time making Mrs. Mahoney and Mr. Jeffries look bad in front of the whole town."

"And that's why he tampered with the salve at the hospital?" Bess asked.

"Right again," I said. "Nathan Emory bragged to him about his big sale of those cheap medicine jars— which weren't authentic, by the way—and Hammond got inspired to poison the salve. Knowing Ms. Waters made it easy for him to show up there to 'help.'"

"The live bullets in his gun," George said. "Was that meant to throw off the reenactment too?"

I nodded, helping myself to more chicken. "Nathan

told Hammond he had some bullets, which gave him the idea. He bought two crates. But then he got scared that I'd find them, so he moved out of our house, broke into the arsenal, and hid them there. It was easy to go the next morning, dressed in a Confederate uniform, and pick up enough to fill his pockets."

"But when we caught him, he was in a Union uniform," George recalled.

"He had two, so he could switch back and forth," I said, "to hide from me and from Pam Mattei. Changing uniforms, he worked his way into a Union cannon crew and set off a cannon ahead of schedule—to launch the battle before things were organized all the way. It created lots of confusion, giving him a chance to sneak around and shoot at Art Jeffries during the battle. I don't think he intended to kill him—he's not a very good shot—but who knows what might have happened by accident?"

"So with all this excitement, Nancy," Dad said, "don't you want to know how the reenactment turned out?"

"Oh, wow, Dad," I said, feeling embarrassed. The biggest event in town, and I had missed most of it while I was down at the police station! "I nearly forgot. Who won?"

"The South, of course." Dad grinned.

Bess balled up her napkin and threw it at him.

"But that was because all the experienced reenactors helped out in the Confederate regiments. It wasn't fair!"

Dad laughed. "No, Bess, it's because the real Confederate army won the real Battle of Black Creek, all those years ago. Reenactments are always faithful to history. Didn't you ever bother to check how the original battle turned out?"

Bess shook her head. "No, Mr. Drew," she admitted, blushing. "I just figured that Colonel Marvin's side won because he was such a hero."

"But next time we'll know," George declared with a grin. She jumped up, ran over to me, and threw her arms around my shoulders. "Figures that the side Nancy Drew decided to fight for won!"